The COLOR

of the

SEASON

By
Julianne MacLean

Prologue

༺ co✑ ༻

Josh Wallace

This past holiday season, I received the greatest gift imaginable—the gift of love. Or maybe it was the gift of life, or wisdom, or a combination of all those things. I'm still not entirely sure. All I know is that I am transformed.

Sometimes I look back on what happened and wonder if it was some kind of stress-induced hallucination. The doctor I told tried to convince me of that, but others were open-minded about my experience and admitted freely that they didn't have all the answers. That what happened to me was outside their realm of experience.

What I am referring to is my unexpected encounter with the afterlife.

Who would have guessed that such remarkable things would happen to a man like me? A cop who carried a gun, never went to church, and considered any type of spiritualism to be silly new age stuff. That was for people who were weak and afraid of the real world, people who needed something else to believe in. Something to help them cope. Or so I thought.

I'll be the first to admit I was naive in that area, and I viewed the world, and my place in it, very superficially.

"What you see is what you get," I used to say.

Who knew there was so much more beneath, and above, the surface of absolutely everything?

A heavy rain was falling when I got out of bed that fateful morning, which seemed fitting, considering I was about to get dumped. I'd felt it in my gut all through the night, churning inside me like a rancid meal. I'd hardly slept a wink.

I rose from bed and stood at the paned window of my Boston flat, watching violent gusts of wind sweep raindrops across the asphalt in the street. Mist rose up from the ground, while leaves on the maple trees along the sidewalk fluttered and the branches swayed.

My body tensed and my head throbbed as I imagined Carla out there somewhere, ignoring my calls.

Because she was with *him*.

What were they doing right now? I wondered irritably. At this very moment?

I bowed my head and leaned forward over the white windowsill, bracing my weight on my knuckles and clenched fists, breathing deep and slow.

Hell. I needed a cup of coffee.

Turning away from the window, I moved into the kitchen to brew a pot, then poured myself a bowl of cereal, which I ate on the sofa while watching the sports channel on television.

I checked my phone again for a text from Carla. Still… nothing.

A part of me wanted to give her the benefit of the doubt, because I knew I wasn't the most rational guy in the world when it came to cheating girlfriends. I'd been burned once before, so I had a small problem with jealousy.

But what if she'd been in a car accident on her way home yesterday and was in a coma at the hospital and couldn't get in touch? If that was the case, I was going to feel pretty guilty.

But it wasn't the case, and I knew it. I'd have heard something.

No, she hadn't texted or called because she didn't know how to tell me it was over. She felt badly about standing me up for dinner the other night and probably wasn't ready to face me and explain herself.

I felt a muscle twitch at my jaw.

Setting my empty cereal bowl down, I rested my elbows on my knees and stared at the blue velvet ring box on the coffee table.

Thirty-five hundred bucks. That's how much that gigantic sucker had cost, and I'd had no choice but to set up a financing plan with monthly payments because I didn't have that kind of cash just sitting around. I probably should have chosen something smaller, but I wanted to make an impression.

Looking back on it, I suppose I thought—with my limited view of the world at the time—that the bigger and flashier the ring, the more tempting my offer would be.

I reached forward to open the box.

Yep, it was one blindingly gorgeous ring. If she could just see it and give me a chance to pop the question…Surely there was still hope. She barely knew the other guy.

In that moment, my phone vibrated with an incoming text. I quickly picked it up.

A half hour later, I opened my front door to find Carla standing on my veranda, shivering in the wind and rain. Her long blond hair was pulled up in a clip at the back, and she looked as classy as ever.

It was astounding, how physically attracted I was to her. Even now.

Especially now.

"Hey," I coolly said. "Come in."

I lived on the second-floor apartment of a century home that had been converted into a rental property, so there wasn't much room in the narrow entrance hall. It certainly wasn't an ideal location to hold a conversation about the rest of our lives together, so I started up the stairs.

"Want a cup of coffee?" I asked, more than a little aware of the chill in my tone, but I couldn't mask it. I was pissed.

"Sure," she replied, unbuttoning her belted trench coat as she followed.

We reached the second level and I went to pour her a cup while she hung her coat and purse on a hook in the hall. By the time she joined me in the kitchen, I was stirring in the cream and sugar.

"Here." I held out the mug.

She accepted it without meeting my gaze and glanced around the apartment. "Thank you."

An ominous silence ensued. The tension was thick as mud.

"Should we go and sit down?" she suggested.

I nodded and gestured toward the sofa in the living room, where we'd spent many evenings wrapped in each other's arms, watching late night movies.

She chose the leather chair by the window, however, which I considered a bad sign.

I sank onto the sofa and watched her sip her coffee. Still she hadn't looked me in the eye. Then, at last, she set the cup down on the table. Naturally, after she called, I'd moved the ring box and placed it in a drawer in my bedroom. At least for now.

"I'm sorry about the other night," Carla said at last. "I hope you were able to cancel the reservations without any trouble."

I shrugged a shoulder. "It's not like they bill you for it."

She nodded and looked down at the floor. "No, of course not."

Another awkward silence rolled through the room, then she cupped her forehead with her hand and shook her head. "God, I'm really sorry, Josh. You're angry with me and you have every right to be. I know things have been...*strained* between us lately."

"Have they?" I asked, needing her to elaborate, because honestly, I'd thought everything was fine. Well, mostly fine. Maybe there was a part of me that knew she didn't belong to me completely, and that's why I'd bought the ring.

Carla let out a sigh. "Yes. I think maybe, we moved a little too fast, right from the beginning. We'd both been through some rough times with relationships that didn't end well, and that's why we wanted so badly for this to work."

"I thought it *was* working," I replied. "And I'm still not convinced it isn't. We've been together almost a year, Carla, and we're good together. You know that. We have great chemistry and we both want the same things—to get married someday and raise a family. Everything was fine until..."

I stopped myself, because I needed to hear *her* say it.

"Until I flew to Canada to be with Seth in the hospital," she replied.

The muscles in my shoulders clenched.

A few months ago, Carla had received a phone call about her late husband, Seth, who had died in a plane crash the year before. But apparently they'd found him alive—or so they thought. In the end, it turned out that the man floating on an iceberg in the middle of the North Atlantic wasn't Carla's husband after all, but some other passenger on the plane who had claimed Seth's belongings.

The man's name was Aaron Cameron—and I wanted to wring his scrawny neck.

Carla sat forward. "I don't know how to explain it, but something happened to me when I was in Newfoundland, and I'm as confused by it as you must be. All I know is that I need to figure this out, and in order to do that, I have to be with Aaron."

My gut squeezed with nausea. I shut my eyes, clenched both hands into fists. "You barely know him. You spent a couple of days with him in the hospital, and now you think he's the great love of your life."

"I'm sorry," she continued in a gentle tone. "I wish you knew how hard this has been for me. I hate doing this, but I don't want to lead you on, or heaven forbid, cheat on you while I figure out what I want."

My eyes flew open. "Figure it out? So you're not even sure?"

She sat back and stared at me. "Like you said, I barely know him, but there's something between us that…" She paused. "I don't know how to explain it, Josh, but it just feels right. It's as if we were meant to find each other and I need to explore that."

Meant to find each other? Seriously?

Reeling with frustration, I rose to my feet and went into the kitchen to pace around for a minute or two. After I cooled the anger in my blood, I returned to the living room and stood on the carpet, facing her.

"We have a good thing here," I said, "but you want to throw it all away for a guy you've only spent a few days with? I thought you were the rational type with both feet on the ground, but maybe I don't know you as well as I thought I did. Maybe the so-called 'magic of the universe' is doing me a favor here, because I sure as hell wouldn't walk away from what we have to go on some ridiculous quest for my *soul mate*. You know I don't believe in that crap, and I sure as hell hope you don't expect me to wait around for you while you go and do that."

She stared at me with something that resembled pity. It only served to piss me off even more.

"I'm sorry you feel that way," she said, "but you're right, I suppose. The universe is doing you a favor, because this isn't meant to be. If it was, everything would be clear. All the pieces would have fallen into place."

"It *was* clear," I reminded her. "At least, it was for me. And you don't really believe that, do you? That the universe will take care of everything? We have to take control of our lives, Carla, and make things happen the way we want them to happen."

"I'm not saying we shouldn't take control," she argued. "I'm just saying that sometimes you have to follow your gut."

"And your gut is telling you that you should run off with a guy you barely know," I reiterated. "That sounds really intelligent." I tapped my forefinger on my temple. "Good to see you're using the old noggin for these major life decisions."

"I'm sorry, Josh. I never meant to hurt you."

Well, you did.

My stomach lurched.

"You can show yourself out," I eventually said.

All the color drained from her face. Then she stood up.

I stepped out of the way to let her pass. Slowly, she collected her coat and purse from the hook on the wall while I stood watching with a tight jaw that made my entire skull throb.

Don't go, I wanted to say. *Please stay. You're making a mistake. We can work this out. I have a ring for you in the other room. Would that change your mind if I offered it to you now?*

But I didn't say any of that, because I had my pride to consider.

Instead I stood in anger, glaring at her while my head pounded with tension.

"I'm very sorry," she said again. "I hope one of these days you'll be able to forgive me."

"Don't bet on it," I replied, and felt an instantaneous regret for lashing out at her that way—at this woman I loved. *Still loved.*

But this was the second time I'd been cheated on, and I was bitter.

I was terribly, terribly bitter.

A few years back, I fell in love with a beautiful woman named Brooke, who I intended to marry. We met in an upscale restaurant downtown not long after I entered the police force. She was fresh out of college, working an entry-level position with a large marketing firm.

I still remember what she wore that night—a skinny black pencil skirt, glossy white blouse, red, patent leather heels. Her black hair was sleek and shiny and hung to a sharp point at her waist. She had an ivory complexion and her smile electrified the whole room. The physical attraction between us was off the charts and we immediately entered into a relationship that lasted well over a year.

All I'd wanted was to be with her forever and maybe that was my problem. I lost sight of everything else in my life. When things eventually settled into a slower pace between us, I wasn't prepared for the possibility that she might get bored.

Which she did.

That became obvious when I invited Kevin, an old college buddy of mine to come and stay with me for the weekend. Brooke soon decided he was far more exciting than I was.

I've since come to realize that she'd always been attracted to men she didn't know very well. I suppose I was in that category when we first met in the restaurant. But when the excitement faded, so did her level of interest.

I walked in on Brooke and Kevin in my apartment, in bed together—which was a double betrayal because Kevin had been one of my best friends since freshman year. I took it pretty hard when he did that to me.

Last I'd heard, he and Brooke dated for about six months, then went their separate ways. I haven't spoken to either of them since, and it was a long time before I felt ready to date again, let alone to enter into another serious relationship. For a while there, I thought I would never be ready.

Until I met Carla.

⁃

I was scheduled to work the graveyard shift on the day Carla dumped me, which at least spared me the agony of going to bed alone, tossing and turning, and over-analyzing what went wrong between us.

I'd done enough of that over the past few days when she stopped answering my calls.

But really…What *had* I done wrong? I was a good guy with a decent job with the Boston Police Department. Sure, I was only an officer in the traffic division, but I was young, educated and ambitious, and I had my eye on the next level. I was confident that eventually I'd slide over to the routine patrol division, learn the ropes there, and sooner or later get promoted to lieutenant. Or I could apply for advanced training for the SWAT unit anytime.

As far as my personal life was concerned, I was as loyal and family-oriented as any man could be. I loved my mom and treated her like a queen. I enjoyed cooking and didn't mind doing dishes and laundry. I'd always loved kids––I certainly had plenty of experience with my nieces and nephews. I adored Carla's teenage daughter Kaleigh and had tried my best to get to know her.

When all was said and done, I had been more than ready to walk down the aisle and become a husband and stepdad. I'd thought Carla wanted that too. I believe she *did* want it.

At least until she flew up to Canada to meet Robinson Crusoe.

Four

As soon as I got into the squad car shortly after midnight and started up the engine, my partner Scott set his coffee in the cup holder and cocked his head.

"So what happened between you and Carla?" he asked. "Did she ever get back to you?"

I shifted into reverse, backed up, and drove out of the station parking lot toward the turnpike.

"Yeah," I replied. "She came over this morning and finally said what needed to be said, so at least now I know."

"Aw, hell," Scott said. "How are you holding up?"

I tugged down on the brim of my hat. "Let's just say I've had better days."

"What about the ring?" Scott asked. "Did you have a chance to give it to her, or at least tell her about it?"

I scoffed. "Are you kidding? After she stood me up and spent the weekend with another guy, I didn't think it was an opportune time."

Scott picked up his coffee and sipped it. "Sorry to hear that. You guys seemed good together. You sure as hell *looked* good, like some Hollywood power couple or something." He paused and glanced out the window while the vehicle tires hissed through puddles on the wet pavement. "But listen—maybe if you tell her about the ring, it might change her mind and make her realize what she's walking away from. You know how girls are about diamonds. The sparkles make them all weepy. My wife practically fainted in my arms when I proposed to her."

"I don't think so," I said, shaking my head. "She seems pretty into the other guy—like she thinks they're soul mates or something, which I really don't get, and I just can't forgive. We've been together for a year. How could she just flick a switch and do an about-face like that?" I waved a hand over the steering wheel. "I really need to let this go. I'm starting to sound like a broken record—a pathetic, heartbroken sap. Somebody, please, just shoot me now."

Scott chuckled. "Hey, I understand. She delivered a blow. Seemed like it came out of nowhere, too." He patted my shoulder. "You'll get through it, buddy. We just need to find you a *new* girl. A really *hot* girl."

I nodded because that was the "guy" thing to do, even though I had no interest in hot new girls. All I wanted was Carla.

"Do you see that?" Scott asked, pointing at the silver minivan in front of us, weaving back and forth over the center line.

Scott called in the license plate number to the dispatcher while I activated the siren and flashing blues.

66 I 'll get this," Scott said, raising the hood of his slicker and opening the car door at the shoulder of the road. "But you could order the rain to stop, if you get a minute."

"Sure thing." I leaned forward slightly to squint up at the dark, overcast sky while water sluiced down over the windshield.

While I kept the wipers moving at full speed and let the car idle to prevent the windows from fogging up, Scott got out and approached the vehicle.

Attentively, I watched him tap a knuckle on the window of the van and begin to converse with the driver. I noted another passenger in front—a woman leaning across the console to speak to Scott, though it was difficult to make her out through the blinking rear tail lights and heavy rain.

Scott eventually moved a few feet back and gestured for the driver to step out of the vehicle.

Must be a DUI, I thought. Not surprising, given how the van was weaving about.

Just as I reached to unfasten my seatbelt, however, I heard a gunshot. I looked up to see Scott stumbling backwards onto the road.

Shit!

Within seconds, I had radioed for backup and was out of the squad car, going for my gun.

"*Freeze! Drop your weapon!*" I shouted, darting a quick glance at Scott. He was conscious and clutching his shoulder.

By now the perp had scrambled back into the minivan. The passenger door opened and the woman fell onto the road, screaming hysterically. "Help me!"

"Stay down!" I shouted at her.

Just as I reached the driver's side door, the tires skidded over the wet pavement, spitting up loose gravel. The van fishtailed out of there.

The next thing I knew, I was aiming my .38 and considering firing off a couple of rounds at the left rear tire, but I didn't have to. The driver hit the brakes for some reason and the minivan did a 180 on the slick pavement. It skidded into the guard rail about a hundred yards away.

"You okay?" I asked Scott, who was rising unsteadily to his feet. I reached out to give him a hand.

"Yeah. The little bastard got me in the arm. I think it just grazed me."

"Get the woman," I said, hearing the sound of the minivan engine sputter. The suspect was attempting to make another escape. "Backup is on the way."

Sirens wailed in the distance. The front door of the van swung open. The suspect hopped out and sprinted down the off-ramp.

"I'm going after him," I said to Scott, and broke into a run.

I barely registered Scott's voice calling after me, telling me to wait for backup. I probably should have listened to him, but I couldn't let the suspect get away. Not after he'd shot my partner at close range.

Running at a fast clip down the off ramp, I radioed in my location and followed the perp into an auto body repair shop parking lot.

I was breathing heavily by then, aware of the sound of my rapid footfalls across the pavement, splashing through puddles.

The suspect disappeared around the back of the building. I followed briskly, pausing at the corner to check my weapon and peer out to make sure he wasn't positioned there, waiting for me.

He had gained some distance and was scrambling up and over a chain-link fence. I immediately resumed my pursuit and climbed the fence to propel myself over.

Inside the repair shop, a dog barked viciously. An outdoor light flicked on, illuminating the rear lot. I was almost over the fence when a door opened and a large German shepherd was released from within. He came bounding toward me, barking and growling.

I dropped to the ground on the other side of the fence.

"Police officer in pursuit of a suspect!" I shouted at the man who followed his dog across the lot.

"He's heading that way!" the man helpfully replied, pointing, but I didn't stop to acknowledge his assistance because the suspect was escaping toward a residential area across the street.

"*Stop! Police!*" I shouted.

To my surprise, just as the shooter reached a low hedge in front of a small bungalow...instead of jumping over it, he halted on the spot and whirled around.

I trained my gun on him. "*Drop your weapon!*"

He raised both arms out to the side.

"*I said drop your weapon!*"

I blinked a few times to clear my vision in the blur of the rain. Then...

Crack!

A searing pain shot through my stomach, just below the bottom of my vest. Then another *crack!* I felt my thigh explode.

Somehow I managed to fire off a few rounds before sinking to the ground. The suspect did the same.

In that instant, two squad cars came skidding around the corner, sirens wailing and lights flashing.

Slowly, wearily, finding it difficult to breathe, I lay down on my back in the middle of the street and removed my hat as I stared up at the gray night sky. A cold, hard rain washed over my face. I began to shiver.

Vaguely, I was aware of the other two units pulling to a halt nearby. I turned my head to watch two officers in raincoats approach the suspect, who was face down in the ditch in front of the hedge.

Then rapid footsteps, growing closer...

"Josh, are you okay?"

I looked up at Gary, a rookie who had offered me a stick of gum in the break room before I'd headed out that night. I nodded my head, but felt woozy. "I think I'm hit."

"Yeah," he replied, glancing uneasily at my abdomen. "Help's on the way. Hang in there, buddy. You're going to be fine."

Feeling chilled to the bone, I shook my head. "I don't think so."

By now Gary was applying pressure to my stomach, which hurt like hell. He shouted over his shoulder, "Need some help over here!"

I clenched my jaw against the burning agony in my guts and leg, and heard more sirens.

"Will they be here soon?" I asked with a sickening mixture of panic and dread.

"Yeah," Gary replied. "Any second now. Just hang on."

"It's cold," I whispered. "I should have worn the raincoat."

More footsteps. I felt no pain, only relief but was drifting off. It was hard to focus.

Another cop knelt down beside me.

I labored to focus on his face.

"MacIntosh," I said. "Can you call Carla for me? Tell her I'm sorry about this morning. Tell her I love her. I didn't mean what I said. I should have walked her to the door."

"You can tell her yourself," MacIntosh replied.

His patronizing response roused a wave of anger in me.

"No." I grabbed his wrist and spoke through clenched teeth. "I need you to promise me...Promise me you'll tell her, or I swear I'll knock your head off."

"All right, all right," he replied. "I'll tell her."

That was the last thing I remembered from that day.

What happened next was strange and incredible. From that moment on, my life became divided into two halves—everything that happened before the shooting, and everything that happened after.

I must have passed out before the ambulance arrived, because I don't remember any of that. I don't recall being placed on a stretcher or speeding to the hospital or being wheeled into the ER—which was probably a good thing because with two bullets in me, I would have been in a lot of pain.

When I finally woke up, there was a team of doctors and nurses crowded around me in an operating room and my stomach was sliced open.

I'd never seen so much blood. They were suctioning it into a tube.

At first, I didn't understand that it was actually *me* on the table. I felt as if I were watching some random operation from over the shoulder of one of the surgeons.

Though I felt sorry for the unfortunate individual on the table. He looked like he was in pretty rough shape.

As the seconds passed, I slowly floated upward until I was hovering close to the ceiling. Only then did I realize that the body on the table was mine and I was not inside it.

Strangely, this didn't trouble me. I was glad not to be in that ravaged body on the table. The whole situation looked rather gruesome. Especially the sounds—the suction machine collecting a seemingly endless supply of blood, the smoky sizzle from the electro cautery, the repetitive clicks and snaps from instruments opening and closing.

"Spleen is shattered," one of the surgeons said. "Grab the artery here, put pressure on it until I can clamp it…Another Kelly, please and zero ties. Keep them coming. We've got lots more bleeders."

I didn't know what any of this meant.

Some kind of alarm went off on one of the beeping monitors and the anaesthetist said, "Doctor"?

I continued to watch with an unemotional curiosity.

"I know, I know," he replied, digging deeper into my guts. He reached in and clamped down on the artery to my spleen. "Zero tie!" He tied furiously. "Mayos." He took the scissors and made a few snips, then pulled out my spleen and dropped it into a steel bin. "This should do it, release the clamp…slowly…"

They all watched in anticipation.

Then blood started to stream again. "Shit."

Another alarm sounded. "We're losing him!" The anaesthetist's voice spoke with urgency as he quickly squeezed a bag of blood into my arm.

I hoped, for their sake, they could work out the problem. As for my own, I didn't really care.

"Get me another six units of PRBCs and FFP."

A nurse ran out of the room. The heart monitor began to hum in a high-pitched, unbroken tone, and everyone moved about in a panic.

"We need chest compressions now. Clamp what you can to stop the bleeding."

The charge nurse dropped the chart to the floor, pulled on a pair of gloves and rushed to help. She began pushing on my chest under the sterile drapes.

The surgeon yelled, "More clamps...now!" as the suction machine rose to a crescendo.

I watched the nurse pump on my chest and understood that I was dying. Oddly, I was indifferent to that. Then I felt a presence behind me. Slowly, I turned.

There was a light in the back corner of the OR. I felt the physical sensation of being drawn toward it. None of this seemed out of the ordinary—not even to me, the most spiritually skeptical person in the universe.

The next thing I remember, after moving through some sort of dark, wide tunnel, was being met by a number of people. Though "people" isn't exactly the right word because they weren't really human. They seemed to be made of light and shadow, so it was impossible to recognize them in a physical sense, though somehow I understood I was with my paternal grandmother.

There were others as well. I might have known some of them...I suspected I did. They felt familiar and intimate, though I couldn't seem to articulate in my mind who they were.

Then the vast, open space all around me began to spin like a tornado. I found myself standing in the center of it, reliving every moment of my life from the time I was born, through childhood and adolescence. I felt everything as if it were happening in real time, except that I could reflect upon it and comprehend every ripple effect of every choice and action—with the wisdom and hindsight of a man who has lived his life a thousand times over.

Or so I thought.

Destiny

ↄ⌒⌒ↄↄ

When I was a kid, I lived with my parents and siblings in a modest white bungalow in a small town on the outskirts of Boston. Back then, there were no cell phones or video game devices in the back pocket of every kid, so we spent a lot of time outdoors, playing street hockey and riding our bikes.

My best friend was a boy named Riley James who lived at the bottom of the cul-de-sac in the biggest, most ostentatious house in the neighborhood: a two story brick colonial with intimidating lion statues flanking the gated driveway.

Riley's dad was a neurosurgeon, so he was hardly ever home, but his mom was really nice. She always invited us in for popsicles and hot dogs in the summer.

Riley had a dog—curiously named Mr. Smith, which always seemed like some kind of alias to me—and a sister named Leah, who was a year and a half older than we were.

We all thought Riley and Leah were insanely rich because they had three televisions, a pool in their backyard, and every February, their parents withdrew them from school to take them to Florida for a week. Riley and Leah came home with enviable golden sun tans and dinky souvenirs for all of us who lived on their street.

For the most part, we were good kids, and our lives were uneventful until, at the age of ten, Riley suggested that he and I take our bikes out to the old Clipper Lake Hotel. It had been abandoned decades earlier and was the subject of much neighborhood gossip.

⤚ᴖ

"What if your dad finds out where we went?" I carefully mentioned as we peddled fast down the dirt road on our bikes.

"No one will know," he replied. "Mom's sick in bed today, and I told her we were biking to Jack's house, and he promised to cover for us. Leah won't say anything."

"Geez, Riley. You told her?" I gritted my teeth with irritation.

"I had to," he shouted defensively. "She got mad when I took the whole box of soda crackers because she wanted them for Mom."

"You could have made something up."

"I know, but I can't think fast on the spot, and besides, Leah always knows when I'm lying. She has some kind of sixth sense."

We rounded a bend and peddled over a wooden bridge. "Do you think she'll rat on us?"

"No way. I promised her a full report, so she'll keep quiet. She's kind of in on it when you think about it because she helped me figure out the map."

"I don't know," I said. "Your sister can be a hard-liner sometimes, just like your dad. I still remember the day she pushed me into the deep end of the pool at the Y. I didn't want to jump and she used her whole body to shove me off the diving board."

Riley laughed. "But you learned how to dive, didn't you?"

We continued peddling along the dirt road, which was muddy in places because it had been a wet spring. The trees were only just beginning to sprout leaves.

"It's farther than I thought it would be," I said. "I just hope we'll make it home before dark or my mom will freak."

"Don't worry," he assured me. "We will."

Just then, we saw a large wooden billboard at the edge of the road, barely visible in the overgrown bush. The paint was peeling, but we were able to read the words:

CLIPPER LAKE HOTEL
STRAIGHT AHEAD .5 MILES

A shiver of anticipation rippled up my spine, followed by a sudden compulsion to turn back, which I fought hard to ignore.

The Clipper Lake Hotel, nestled on the woodsy shore of a large freshwater lake, had been built in 1902. According to legend, it had dominated the area for decades as the premier summer resort for the wealthy residents of Boston.

It was the kind of place that was given a fresh coat of white paint each year. It boasted a large wraparound veranda with dozens of wicker chairs and tables with chintz cloths. The ladies sipped lemon iced tea and fanned themselves on hot summer afternoons, while the gentlemen ordered brandy and talked about politics in the library. There were a number of small private cottages as well, stretched along the pebbled shoreline.

It was especially popular with honeymooners, but Riley and I had heard from a girl in the eighth grade that when a new owner took over in the 1970s, he installed a bunch of heart-shaped beds and shiny red hot tubs. After that, it lost most of its historic charm, the rates went down, and gradually it became the premier party location for drug users.

Sadly, it shut down in 1986 when one of the guests went on a shooting rampage and killed nine people, including the owner's wife. Six months later, the owner declared bankruptcy and hung himself from one of the beams in the basement.

It was a dark and tragic tale, but Riley and I were just kids and we couldn't truly comprehend the reality of it.

In any case, what lured us to the lake that day was something else entirely. We were most fascinated by the stories about the ghosts—because according to rumor, the place was splendidly haunted.

—⟶

It was long past noon when we peddled onto the weedy, deserted parking lot. As soon as the building came into view, I hit my brakes and skidded to a halt. Riley did the same.

Together we looked across at the once majestic hotel, now a beastly monstrosity with a sagging roof and rotting gray clapboard. Only the smallest traces of white paint remained as evidence of its former glory.

Off to the side, in the field next to a dilapidated swing set, was a rusted-out, broken-down car with bullet holes in it.

"Wow," Riley said. "This looks amazing."

"Are you sure we should go in?" As soon as the words passed my lips, I regretted them.

Riley turned to me with an accusing glare. "Are you chicken?"

"No," I quickly professed. "I just don't want to get arrested, that's all."

He rolled his eyes. "We won't get arrested, nimrod. It's not like the cops ever get called out here. Come on, let's go."

Not wanting to appear a coward, I followed Riley to the main entrance, where we got off our bikes and stood them up on their kickstands.

For a brief moment I hoped that the place would be locked up tighter than a state prison and we'd have to settle for peering in the windows, but all the windows had been boarded up long ago, then ripped off by vandals. The ornate, heavy oak entrance doors were knocked off their hinges, so there was nothing but air to keep us out.

"Do you think anyone's here?" I asked.

"I sure hope not," Riley replied.

He entered first, stepping over the fallen door, and I followed him into the main lobby.

It was difficult to imagine what it might have looked like in its heyday. Now, the wallpaper was faded and torn away; the walls and ceilings were covered in cobwebs and graffiti; and the spindles on the main staircase railing had been kicked out.

What was most unsettling, however, was the silence of the place. Outside of my own breathing, there were no sounds of humanity, not even the hum of an air conditioner or refrigerator or the faint roar of traffic in the distance. It felt as if we had crossed over into another dimension.

A pigeon fluttered out of a hole in the wall, flapping its wings wildly and flying out through the main door. Riley and I both jumped as the bird sailed past.

"Geez! That scared me!" Riley shouted. "Come on. Let's go check out some of the rooms. I wonder if they still have beds in them."

"If they do, they'll probably be crawling with bugs," I replied, following him up the stairs. "It smells musty."

We reached the second floor and started down the long, narrow corridor where more graffiti covered the walls. As we pushed our way through a few more cobwebs, my heart pounded heavily in my chest. I kept expecting something to jump out at me—something far worse than a pigeon.

"No wonder they say it's haunted," Riley said. "It's really creepy. I wonder where the shootings happened." He peered into the first room we came to with an old bed, no mattress.

"There's hardly any furniture," I said. "Everything from the old hotel would be antiques by now, probably worth a lot of money. I wonder if people stole stuff over the years."

"That's probably what happened. Or maybe the owners sold it."

We stepped gingerly over the creaky floorboards and checked out each room on either side of the corridor until we came to the end of the hall.

"This door must have been added later," Riley said. "It doesn't look old like everything else."

"It's a fire door," I explained, pushing the handle to open it. "They probably had to add this stairwell when the rules changed about having proper exits."

"Want to go up a level?" Riley asked.

"Sure."

In all honesty, I preferred the modern metal staircase to the rest of the hotel. It made me feel like we were back in a more familiar world.

The heavy door slammed shut behind us, and I jumped when it echoed loudly. Then I noticed a bad smell and covered my nose with a hand.

We climbed one flight and reached another door with the number three painted on it. I turned the knob.

"Shoot," I said. "This one's locked. We'll have to go back down."

"Let's go up first," Riley said. "Maybe the fourth floor will be open.

There was only one window at the very top to light the stairwell. The two of us hurried up, taking two steps at a time to reach door number four.

That, too, was locked.

A rush of nervousness filled my belly.

"Are they all locked?" Riley asked with concern, tugging violently at the knob with both hands. He proceeded to kick the door a bunch of times.

By now I was already on my way back down. "It's a fire exit," I said, "so there has to be a way out. That's the whole point of having them. There should be a push handle on the ground floor."

I hurried down. The lower I went, the darker it got. This made me run faster.

When I reached the ground floor, I didn't stop. I ran straight into the steel door and shoved myself up against the horizontal exit bar. It refused to open. I tried and tried, but it was no use.

"What's going on?" Riley asked when he appeared behind me. "Is this one locked too? I thought you said it would open."

"It should," I ground out, still fighting with it. "I think there must be something wedged up against it on the outside."

"Like what?"

"I don't know, but it must be something heavy. Help me push."

The two of us thrust our shoulders up against the door for what seemed like an eternity, but it wouldn't budge.

Finally, Riley sat down on the steps. "Are we locked in here?"

I checked under the stairs to see if there was another exit, but all I found was a cement wall. "No, there has to be a way out."

I stepped around Riley and climbed back up to the second floor where we had come in. That door was still locked, as were all the others. The window at the top didn't open at all. It was made of wire mesh, and even if it did open, it was a four-storey drop straight down.

"What are we going to do?" Riley asked in a panic, meeting me on my way back down.

I paused with my hand on the railing. "I don't know, but I think we're in big trouble."

⸺ᡍ⸺

For the next few hours, we continued to fight with all the doors and even tried kicking through the walls, but they seemed to be made of cement. Picking the locks wasn't an option either, because we had nothing on us that would fit into the keyholes.

By late afternoon, the sun dropped low in the sky and we sat down on the steps, exhausted.

"My dad's going to kill me," Riley said. "He's going to chew me up and spit me out on the front lawn."

"Mine too," I replied, though I doubted I'd have it as bad as Riley, because his father was worse than an army drill sergeant.

Every morning before Riley and Leah left for school, their beds had to be made with hospital corners and without creases. If they were ever caught leaving a dirty dish anywhere in the house, or not hanging up their jackets when they came in the door, they had to do extra chores for a week. There were more rules about grades and Riley had a hard time with that because he wasn't as book smart as Leah.

"I guess it's a good thing you told Leah where we were going," I said. "At least somebody knows where we are."

"But she'll get in trouble too," he said, "just for keeping it secret all day."

"Maybe your dad won't come home tonight and he won't even know," I suggested.

"How's that supposed to work?" Riley asked. "The minute I don't show up for supper, Mom's going to start calling people."

"At least somebody will come and get us," I said. "Even if we get grounded for a year, it would be better than spending the night in here."

Little did we know, Riley's mom was still throwing up at supper time, so my mom had to take her to the clinic—which meant no one was home at either of our houses to even notice we were gone.

By the time the sun went down, we were huddled together on the fourth-floor landing, surrounded by pitch black, waiting for someone to find us. At the time, I told myself there were no such things as ghosts, but now, after everything I've been through, I'm not sure I was right.

I had no idea what time it was when my eyes flew open in the darkness.

"What was that?" I asked with fright, sitting up from my fetal position on the landing.

"What was *what*?" Riley asked.

"You didn't see it? A flash of light? It moved across the ceiling."

"Are you sure?" he replied.

"I don't know." *Was I dreaming this?*

We both scurried on our backsides into the corner under the window.

"Do you hear anything?" Though I spoke in a whisper, the sound of my voice seemed to echo up and down the stairwell.

"No. Do you?" Riley replied.

I shook my head and hugged my knees to my chest. "It's so dark in here. This must be what it's like to be blind. I wish we knew what time it was."

I wanted to know how long it would be before the sun would come up. If we could just survive until then...

Then *whoosh*! Another flash of light swept across the ceiling.

"There! See?"

"Maybe it's lightning," Riley whispered shakily. "Maybe we'll hear thunder in a second."

I counted out loud—one second for every mile—but reached twenty and there was nothing. Just silence when I stopped counting.

Riley grabbed hold of my arm. "What are we going to do?"

"Just sit here and be really quiet," I replied. "The light can't hurt us."

"But what if it's more than just a light?" he asked. "What if it's a ghost and he wants to murder us?"

"There's no such thing as ghosts," I assured him, trying hard to believe it myself, which was no easy task through my blinding terror.

"Then why'd you come out here with me?" Riley asked. "If you didn't believe in ghosts?" He sounded like he was on the verge of tears.

"I don't know. I just thought it would be a cool thing to do."

Suddenly, there was a voice in the distance. It was crying out for help.

"What's that?" Riley clutched my hand and squeezed it so hard, he cut off the blood supply to my fingers. There was an unexpected, loud crashing sound and we both screamed our lungs out as light filled the stairwell.

"Riley James? Josh Wallace?" someone shouted.

We both fell silent at the sound of our names. Heavy footsteps pounded up the stairs. The beam of light traveled jerkily up the wall.

Slowly coming to realize that it was not a ghost, but a flesh-and-blood human being moving toward us, I leaped to my feet. "We're here!" I squinted and shaded my eyes against an intense spotlight.

"Hello boys," the woman said good-naturedly. Immediately I realized she was a female police officer. "Your parents have been pretty worried about you."

All the breath sailed out of my lungs. *We were saved!*

Bending forward, I fought to hold back the urge to vomit, while Riley sprang to his feet and dashed straight into the police-woman's arms.

⤳

"You really saved our bacon," I said to Leah after we got out of the cop car in front of Riley's house. It was almost midnight and both our mothers had squeezed the daylights out of us and wept tears of joy.

Leah folded her arms. "You might not think so later when my dad gets home. He was in the middle of a surgery when they told him you two were missing. My mom's been a nervous wreck ever since we got home from the doctor."

We both looked over at Mrs. James, who was still talking to the police officer.

"How is she?" I asked, thinking of how sick she'd been all day.

"Turns out she didn't have the stomach flu after all," Leah replied. "She's pregnant."

My eyebrows lifted. "Really?"

Leah moved closer and lowered her voice. "I heard her talking to the nurses. She's afraid to tell Dad because they were supposed to be all done having kids. They only planned to have two."

"So it was an accident?" I whispered.

Leah nodded. "Dad's not going to like that. Not one little bit."

Again, I glanced over at Mrs. James, who'd always been such a great mom to all of us on the street. I couldn't imagine she wouldn't be happy about having another baby.

The cops got into their car and drove off. As soon as they disappeared around the corner, a shiny black car entered the neighbourhood and pulled into the driveway. It was Leah's father.

"Oh great," she said with a sigh. "You should probably go home, Josh."

I felt like a deer caught in the headlights as Dr. James got out and slammed the car door. He strode purposefully across the lawn and smacked Riley hard across the face.

"Ow!" Riley cried, holding his cheek with a hand while Mrs. James covered her mouth.

"Get in the house!" Dr. James shouted. "Right now!"

Everyone fell silent.

When Dr. James reached the steps, he turned and pointed a finger at me. "As for you, Josh Wallace, I don't want you coming around here anymore. Do you understand me? You're nothing but trouble. Stay away from my kids. *Leah!* Get in the house! *Now!*"

Leah ran inside and Dr. James followed her in.

My mother slowly approached Mrs. James and touched her shoulder. "Everything will be all right," she gently whispered. "Maybe wait a few days before you tell him your happy news."

"*Happy* news?" She shook her head. "I don't think he's going to see it that way. Maybe I won't tell him at all."

My mother considered that for a moment. "A baby's not something you can keep secret forever, Margie."

Mrs. James shot her a desperate look. "Isn't it?" She turned and strode to the door.

We watched until she disappeared, then my mom gathered me into her arms. "Don't worry, Josh. You'll still be able to play with Riley and Leah again. Their father's just angry because he was worried. He'll get over it."

"I don't know, Mom. He looked pretty serious."

As we turned to walk home under the hazy glow of the neighborhood streetlights, I took hold of my mother's hand. "What did she mean about keeping the baby a secret from Dr. James? How could she do that?"

My mother hesitated before answering the question. "She'll come around. She'll find the right time to tell him and everything will be fine."

Though my mom didn't explain what, exactly, Mrs. James was contemplating, I was old enough to have learned a few things and I was pretty sure I understood what she meant.

"I hope she has the baby," I said, glancing over my shoulder at the showy brick house at the end of the street. "I'll be sad if she doesn't."

We went inside our modest little bungalow, where Mom sat me down at the kitchen table. She asked if I was hungry. Naturally I said yes.

"How about a grilled cheese sandwich? I promise, nothing tastes better than a grilled cheese when you've had a rough day."

"Okay."

While my mom stood at the stove with a spatula, watching over the cast iron frying pan, I told her all about the old Clipper Lake Hotel and how we got locked in the stairwell.

A short while later, when I bit into that crispy, buttery grilled sandwich, I was never so happy to be home...and to be a member of this family, and no other.

Meanwhile, down the street, major decisions were being made—decisions that were about to affect the course of all our lives.

For a full week after what came to be known as The Great Haunted Stairwell Incident, I didn't see a trace of Riley or Leah in the neighborhood or at school. I called their home many times, but no one answered.

I could never tell if Mrs. James was at home because she always parked her car in the garage and the only window was covered by a blind with the louvers down.

I did notice Dr. James's car pass by on the street a few times, very late at night, which wasn't unusual. He often came home late from surgeries at the hospital.

My mom also tried calling Mrs. James, but no one ever picked up the phone. Eventually she grew worried enough to march down the street herself and ring the doorbell. The housekeeper answered and told her that Mrs. James had taken the children away to stay with their grandparents in Arizona for the week. Mom then proceeded to sweetly wrestle the Arizona number out of the unsuspecting housekeeper. She came straight home and dialed the number, just to make sure everyone was all right.

"It's not fair," I said to Mom when I came home from school that day and heard the news. "He's my best friend."

"I know it's difficult," she replied, "but they're not moving to the moon. Only to Boston. It's less than an hour away."

"It's not because of me, is it?" I asked. "Because you heard what Dr. James said—that he didn't want me coming around anymore. Is this my fault? Am I the reason they're moving?"

"Of course not," Mom replied with compassion, stroking my hair away from my forehead. "He was wrong to say that to you. He was just frightened and upset and he wanted someone to blame."

"It wasn't even my idea to take our bikes to the hotel," I said irritably. "It was Riley's."

"I know." She poured me a glass of milk and brought me a peanut butter cookie, which I ate in silence while she peeled carrots at the counter.

"Will they come home before they move?" I asked. "Will we ever see them again?"

"I'm not sure, honey," she replied. "We'll have to wait and see."

As it turned out, Mrs. James and her children never set foot in our neighborhood again. Mom nevertheless made an effort to keep in touch with Mrs. James, and I was allowed to talk to Riley and Leah on the phone a few times over the summer while they were staying with their grandparents in Arizona.

Riley always asked if I would ever go back to the Clipper Lake Hotel. He wanted me to find out what was wedged up against the door of the fire exit. He said it still bothered him that we'd been locked inside. He confessed he was having nightmares about it.

He asked if I was having nightmares, too.

I said no—because I didn't believe in ghosts. I explained to him that the light we saw move across the ceiling of the stairwell was the beam from the police officer's flashlight. They had been walking around outside the hotel, shining lights along the windows.

But the part about not believing in ghosts...?

Well, maybe I did believe, because I'd woken up in a state of panic more than once that summer, drenched in sweat, my chest heaving when I thought there was some unearthly presence standing over my bed, watching me in the darkness.

If there was a presence, was it there to protect me? Or lead me somewhere?

By the time September rolled around, an older couple without any children had moved into the big brick house on our cul-de-sac. Riley and Leah had moved to Boston to live in an even larger Victorian mansion their father had purchased for them while they were in Arizona. They were enrolled in an expensive private school which required them to wear uniforms and play instruments in the school band.

Sadly, for the remainder of that year, we lost touch completely.

I still managed to keep busy, however, by trying out for the basketball team and working a little harder at my studies. Mom organized more than the usual number of family events, and we even took a trip up to Six Flags the week before Thanksgiving.

Before we knew it, it was time to start decorating for the holidays. I ventured into the season with an eagerness and impatience that confounded me because it was unmatched by any previous holiday season of my young life.

Even then, as a boy of ten, I was puzzled by my anticipation, since I'd stopped believing in Santa Clause and there wasn't really anything special I wanted under the tree.

Nevertheless, each morning I woke with a quiet excitement that simmered in my body. With tremendous care, I peeled open another tiny window on my Advent calendar. At night, I stared at the calendar's nativity scene with fascination until I drifted off to sleep.

There were no more nightmares after that.

When Christmas Day arrived at last, my brothers, sisters and I woke at dawn to giant white snowflakes floating buoyantly down from the sky. I remember feeling mesmerized and strangely euphoric as I watched them from my bedroom window.

Later that morning—after we finished opening gifts and had stuffed ourselves with pancakes, bacon, and egg nog—my mother received an unexpected phone call.

I don't know how, but I knew it was something important. *Something momentous.* I could tell by the way she set her coffee cup down on the kitchen counter and turned quickly toward me.

"It's Mrs. James," she said with an unsettling urgency. "She's calling from Massachusetts General Hospital."

Despite the fact that it was Christmas morning and we were expected at my grandmother's house for turkey dinner at 4:00, my mother hung up the phone and told me to get dressed.

"Why?" I asked, feeling almost afraid to hope.

"Because we're driving into the city to see Riley and Leah." Her whole face lit up with a smile. "And their new baby sister!"

My eyes opened wide. "Really?"

"Yes!" She moved closer to hug me. "Mrs. James had the baby at daybreak this morning and she's doing very well. The kids are with her now and she said they miss you, especially today. They practically begged her to call us."

I missed them, too, because Riley, Leah and I had known each other since we were toddlers. We always got together every Christmas morning to play with our new toys.

"When can we go?" I asked.

"Right now," she replied. "But we'll need to leave soon if we're going to make it back in time for dinner."

I immediately went to my room to get dressed.

∽

Because it was Christmas, there was no traffic on the roads, which enabled us to reach the hospital in record time. According to my new stopwatch—a special gift from my grandmother—it took us exactly forty-three minutes to travel from door to door.

"What a perfect Christmas Day," Mom said as we got out of the car and looked up at the sky. Fat snowflakes had begun to fall again and everything in the city was covered in white. I felt like I was standing inside a snow globe.

"I can't wait to see Riley," I said as I reached for the gift bag in the back seat. The gift, however, was not for him, but for the new baby. Since there were no stores open to purchase anything, I'd suggested that we re-wrap the soft green bunny I'd received from my aunt that morning.

Not that I didn't appreciate the gift. It was cute and cuddly with floppy ears, but weren't bunnies meant for girls?

My mom felt it would be a nice gesture, so I called my aunt and explained the circumstances. She agreed it was a nice idea.

A short while later, we stepped off the elevator on the neo-natal floor and asked to see Mrs. James. Before the nurse had a chance to reply, I heard the familiar sound of Leah's voice, calling to me.

"*Josh!*"

I turned, and there she stood at the end of the long corridor wearing a white sweater-dress that sparkled under the florescent hospital lights. Her long brown hair was pulled back in a pony-tail, and she'd sprouted a few inches. I was stunned by how grown up she appeared.

How was it possible that this girl I'd known since I was in diapers could be so unrecognizable to me?

She looked like an angel. I couldn't seem to make my mouth work.

Then she began to run the length of the corridor, and when she reached me, she threw her arms around my neck. "I'm so happy to see you!"

"Me, too," I managed to reply. "Merry Christmas."

She drew back and regarded me joyfully. "Merry Christmas to you, too. Hi, Mrs. Wallace. We're glad you could come. My mom can't wait to see you." Leah backed away and beckoned to us with a hand. She seemed to move in slow motion. "Follow me. It's this way, just at the end of the hall. Wait until you see the baby. She's the most beautiful thing in the whole wide world. Josh, you're going to *love* her."

Mom and I followed her into a private room where Mrs. James was sitting up on a bed, smiling. I'd never seen her look so happy.

My mom immediately rushed to her side and hugged her. While they gushed and cried over seeing each other again and talked animatedly about the labor and delivery, I spotted Riley, lounging at his ease against the window sill.

"Hi," I said with a casual wave of my hand.

"Hi back," he replied, flipping his hair out of his eyes.

"How's it going?"

He shrugged. "All right I guess. How's school?"

"Same as always. Mr. Gillespie is still talking about bugs in bio class, and Joanie Carruthers is still chasing after Nick Saunders."

Looking bored, Riley slowly nodded, then turned his eyes toward the window again.

I felt Leah touch my arm. "Want to hold the baby?" she asked.

A shiver of elation moved through me as I turned to face her. There in her arms was her newborn baby sister, bundled up in white flannel. Leah regarded me with excitement.

"I don't know," I replied, taking a clumsy step back.

My mother quickly took notice of my unease. "Go ahead, Josh. There's a chair behind you. You can hold her on your lap."

I glanced down at a sturdy oak rocker with a yellow flowered cushion. "All right."

Setting the gift bag on the floor, I sat down and held my arms out to Leah. Her green eyes held me entranced. There was something wise and all-knowing about the way she looked at me. I felt suddenly weightless, like those snowflakes floating in the air outside the window.

Then slowly...carefully...she laid the sleeping infant in my arms.

The baby was tightly swaddled and I found it surprisingly easy to cradle her. I shifted a bit to find a more comfortable position, then began to rock back and forth in the chair.

"What's her name?"

"We don't know yet," Leah replied. "Mom was thinking about calling her Amy, but now that we've met her, we don't think that's the right name." Leah pointed at the gift bag on the floor. "Is this for her?"

I nodded.

Leah turned to her mother. "Can we open it?"

"Of course," Mrs. James replied.

Leah bent to pick it up and removed the pink tissue paper. "It's a bunny," she said, lifting the toy out of the bag. "Look, Mom." She carried it to her mother so she could feel how soft it was, then she returned to my side. "She's going to *love* it."

My eyes lifted to meet Leah's, and my pulse slowed to a calm and steady pace. A deep feeling of peace settled over me, as if all was now right with the world.

Leah smiled. I was immensely grateful to be with her again. I didn't want to move. I didn't want her to go. I wanted to stay right there in that perfect place.

Forever.

"*Open your eyes, Josh,*" she whispered.

My forehead crinkled in a frown. I didn't understand why she would say that to me. What did she mean?

"*Can you hear me?*"

A light flashed, just like the flashlight beam across the ceiling in the hotel stairwell.

Then the room began to spin.

Around and around it went, until I felt a massive jolt.

Awakening

avaged. That's how I felt.

Pain exploded through my central core and shot down the length of my left thigh. This was followed by a searing burst of panic that radiated outward from my heart.

I could feel but I could not see. I was totally blind.

Or maybe I was blind because I hadn't yet resolved the issue of how to open my eyes.

Open, damn you!

My mind screamed the command, but my lids merely fluttered in response. My frustration mounted.

A flash of light swept through the darkness.

Fear and confusion gripped me.

"Josh, can you hear me? I know you can do it. Wake up. Wake up."

I fought with all my might against the stubborn weight of my eyelids. Then at last they lifted, and I saw a hand in front of my face. It held a penlight. The light was sweeping back and forth. Everything was blurry.

"That's it," the voice whispered with encouragement. "You can do it."

It was a woman.

Leah...?

No. That wasn't possible.

The penlight clicked off and the room became bathed in semi-darkness again as I watched that mysterious hand slip the little black device into the breast pocket of a white lab coat.

"I'm right here, Josh," she said. "You're doing great."

I struggled to focus on what was in front of me…a pair of achingly familiar green eyes blinking down at me. *Was I still dreaming? Or was this death?*

Every instinct in my body told me it was Leah, but the world was still a blur and I couldn't let myself believe it. This had to be a lingering imprint from all those memories that had flashed through my mind.

"Am I dead?" I asked.

She smiled and laughed, but there were tears in her eyes. "No, but you came pretty darn close. Welcome back to the world of the living. Good decision, by the way."

She wiped a tear from her cheek with the back of her hand.

"Leah?" I whispered, still unable to believe she was truly standing over me. *How was this possible? Was I really alive?*

"You can see me?" she asked as if she couldn't believe it either. "Can you hear me?"

I managed a nod.

"Then this has to be some kind of miracle," she said.

I blinked a few times, then glanced at the name tag on her lab coat. It said Dr. Leah James.

"You work here?" I ground out.

She nodded. "I'm a third year psychiatry resident. I shouldn't really be in here with you. I'm supposed to be somewhere else right now, but when I saw them take you out of the ambulance…" Her voice quavered. "I couldn't believe it was you and I had to stay with you. It's been such a long time, Josh." She glanced over her shoulder at the door. "There's a nurse coming in now and the ICU doc should be right behind her. I really should go."

I couldn't think straight. I felt frazzled and displaced.

Then I remembered watching the details of my operation. My stomach was open...There was blood everywhere...a warm light and a tunnel that pulled me in...

"Will you come back?" I asked.

I wanted to tell her what had happened to me. Would she believe it? Would anyone believe it?

Leah hesitated, then nodded. "I will, but right now they need to check you over. You did really well, Josh. You're a survivor, I'll give you that. I'm so glad you made it."

Just then, a nurse ran into the room. She flicked on the lights which startled me. Leah blew me a kiss as she backed away and discreetly passed by the nurse on her way out.

⌒⌒⌒

"How long was I out?" I asked Dr. Crosby, who leaned over me to listen to my chest with a stethoscope. He was an older, heavyset man with white hair, bushy eyebrows and gold spectacles. He ignored my question as he focused on his task. After a moment, he tugged the ear buds out and looped the instrument around his neck.

"You've been in a coma for five days," he replied as he checked both my incisions, "so let me be the first to congratulate you on what has been an amazing recovery. You're a real fighter, Josh. There's no doubt about that."

I grimaced slightly and spoke in a hoarse whisper. "Thank you."

"Any trouble catching your breath?" he asked.

"No."

"Chest pain? Pain in your calves?"

"My thigh's pretty sore."

He turned to the nurse. "Get him some Dilaudid. Two milligrams. Slow IV push." He held a finger up in front of my face. "Now I want you to follow my finger with your eyes. Any double vision?"

"No."

"Good. Now look at my nose." He shone a penlight in both my eyes. "Very good." Leaning back, he dropped the light into his pocket. "Squeeze my fingers as hard as you can. Excellent, Josh." He told me to lift my good leg. "Now try to resist while I push down."

While he checked my reflexes, I asked, "What happened to me…exactly?"

It was a pretty broad inquiry, considering all the questions I had about the past five days.

He peered at me curiously over the rims of his spectacles. "Josh, do you remember *anything* about what occurred?"

Feeling tired all of a sudden, I closed my eyes. "I know I was wounded while pursuing a suspect. He shot me in the stomach and the leg."

"Good," the doctor said.

I opened my eyes and turned my head on the pillow. "Did you just say 'good'?"

He chuckled. "I meant it's good that you remember what happened. And do you know where you are? What city?"

"I'm in the hospital, and this is Boston." I took a few seconds to draw in a breath. "Is my partner okay? What about the woman in the van? Do you know anything about that?"

"I'm afraid not," Dr. Crosby said. "But I'm sure your colleagues will be in to see you in the morning. Your family's been here constantly. Tonight was the first night none of them stayed, only because the nurses badgered them to go home and get some rest." He consulted the clipboard and flipped one of the pages over the back. "Oh, and your girlfriend was here as well."

My pulse hammered against the inside of my veins. "Girlfriend?"

"Yes. Blond hair. Nice smile. She had a daughter with her…"

"Carla?"

He wrote something down on the chart. "I'm not sure what her name was. You'd know better than I would."

I swallowed uneasily and wondered if Carla had changed her mind about us. Maybe the thought of losing me—*really* losing me—had caused her to rethink her decision. Or did she just feel guilty?

Dr. Crosby circled around the bed and checked something on one of the monitors. While he was doing that, the nurse returned and administered what I assumed to be pain medication. I immediately relaxed as it flowed through my system.

"Can I ask you something?" I said to the doctor, turning my head on the pillow.

"Sure." He seemed distracted by what he was writing in my chart.

"Did my heart stop while I was in the operating room?"

That caused him to look up. He inclined his head slightly. "Why would you ask that?"

I wasn't sure how to explain because I didn't want to come off as a nutcase, but I needed to know what happened.

"I think I had a…" I paused and spoke in a whisper. "I'm not sure what to call it. It was some kind of experience, I guess."

"What kind of experience?"

My mouth went dry. "This is going to sound crazy. I don't even know if it was real. Maybe it was just a dream. Or maybe it was one of those…You know…"

He shook his head and leaned a little closer.

I glanced over at the nurse, who appeared busy with something. "It might have been one of those near-death experiences." I whispered, "*I saw a light.*"

For a moment the doctor studied my pupils. "What kind of light?"

"I'm not sure how to describe it. It was...peaceful. It drew me in."

"What else did you see, Josh?"

Terrific. He did think I was a nut. I could hear it in his voice.

I probably should have shrugged it all off right there and said it was just a dream. It must have been the drugs that made me continue to blabber on because I was pretty sure that when I sobered up from all this, I wouldn't want the guys at the station to hear about it.

"I saw the operation," I told him, "but it was like I was watching from the ceiling. One of the surgeons said they were losing me, and everyone panicked. Is that what happened? Did I flatline?"

"I wasn't there," Dr. Crosby replied, "so I'm not sure about the details."

Wouldn't it be in the chart? I wondered.

He patted me on the shoulder. "Rest assured, you're fine now. The surgery went well and they were able to remove both bullets."

"What about my spleen?" I asked. "They removed that too, didn't they?"

There was no way I could miss how the nurse stopped what she was doing and looked up to meet Dr. Crosby's eyes.

"They did." He moved around the bed and spoke quietly to the nurse. "Let's order a psych consult for tomorrow."

Can you at least send for the third year resident with the long brown hair?

Leah.... I want Leah.

The drugs were making me sleepy...

"Everything else looks good," Dr. Crosby cheerfully said. "Now you just need to focus on healing. First thing tomorrow, we'll set you up in a physio program."

"Physio?" I drowsily asked.

"For your leg," he explained. "The bullet went straight into a major muscle. Tore it up pretty bad. I'm afraid you'll be off work for a while."

"How long?"

"At least six weeks, I'd say."

Six weeks?

Ah, hell. That wasn't what I wanted to hear because I'd been busting my butt lately to get a promotion.

"Will I make a full recovery?" I groggily asked. I certainly didn't want to end up walking with a cane, stuck behind a desk before I could really prove myself in the field.

Though maybe I'd already done that with this fiasco.

"That's entirely up to you," the doctor replied as he lowered the clipboard to his side, "and how hard you're willing to work at this. I'll warn you now, though—it's not going to be easy. There will be pain, but you seem to be made of pretty stern stuff. You just have to make up your mind every day—are you going to throw in the towel, or are you going to throw one more punch?"

"A boxing metaphor," I said with a sigh, gazing up at the ceiling, still thinking about Carla, wondering why she had come.

"Just remember," he said, "half the battle's up here." He tapped his temple three times with the tip of his finger.

"I'll keep that in mind."

"Good for you. Now I have to go take care of a few things. This is Nurse Gayle. She'll answer any other questions you might have."

She leaned over the bed and smiled at me.

I had so many questions about what happened, I didn't know where to begin—but it wasn't Nurse Gayle I wanted to talk to.

I fell asleep again not long after the nurse left, and woke the next morning when an orderly came in to deliver a breakfast tray. He adjusted my bed so I could sit up and rolled the tray table across my lap. I took one look at the cup of broth and the tiny bowl of green Jell-O.

"This is all I get? I haven't eaten in five days. I'm starved."

"The doctor wrote DAT in your chart," he informed me, "which means 'diet as tolerated.' They'll see how you do sipping on this, then they'll advance you to something more."

"So lunch will be better?"

"Maybe. As long as you can keep this down."

"Great." I reached for the cup of broth and hoped for the best.

A half hour later, my mother, stepdad and sister, Marie, walked into the room. Mom burst into tears at the sight of me.

"Thank God!" she said, bending over the bed rail to hug me. "I'm so sorry we weren't here when you woke up. I'll never forgive myself."

"No worries, Mom. You're here now."

Marie moved to the other side of the bed and hugged me as well. "You are one tough cop," she said with a grin. "Too bad you missed all the hoopla. You were all over the news."

"Yeah?" I replied, shaking Eric's hand. "So I'm a celebrity now?"

"Pretty much," Marie replied. "The reporters were outside for the first few days, but they're gone now. I'm sure they'll be back when they hear you're awake."

I rubbed the back of my neck. "I'm not really up for talking to reporters. I haven't even tried to walk yet. And I could use a shower."

"Don't worry about any of that press stuff," Marie said. "We'll handle everything and tell them how you're doing. There are a lot of concerned people out there, you know. All kinds of flowers were left out front. People were lighting candles and praying for you constantly."

I thought about my strange experience in the operating room and couldn't help but wonder if it was all those prayers that had brought me back. I probably should have said something to my family about what occurred, but for some reason that morning, it seemed less real than it had when I first woke up to the bright pen light shining in my eyes.

Maybe it *was* just a dream. Maybe *that* was the light I saw...

"Have you talked to anyone yet?" Marie asked.

I laced my fingers together on my lap. "About what?"

"About what happened when you were shot. Did you know the carjacker's in custody?"

"He's alive?" I was relieved to hear it.

"Yeah, he's fine. You shot him in the leg and he was released from the hospital after a day or two."

"What about Scott?"

"He's fine, too," Marie replied. "He was lucky the guy had such terrible aim. It was just a surface wound on his arm. The woman is okay and feeling very grateful for what you and Scott did for her. She said the carjacker stole her van while she was pumping gas. He forced her inside, then got behind the wheel and kept the gun on her. Turns out he was running from some drug dealers he owed money to. The woman came to visit you a few days ago. Those are the flowers she left."

Marie pointed toward the window.

"That was thoughtful," I said.

Mom leaned over the bed to kiss me on the cheek. "We're just glad you're all right. We've all been so worried."

She stepped back when two nurses entered the room with towels and a pan of water. "Good morning, Officer Wallace," one of them said cheerfully. "I'm Terri. Are you ready for a bath?"

"I thought you'd never ask," I replied.

My family went for coffee.

～

After a light lunch of vegetable soup and more Jell-O, which I kept down without any trouble, the two young nurses returned to coax me out of bed and take me for a walk down the hall.

"The sooner we get you moving the better," Nurse Becky said as she lowered the bedrail. "It's been five days since your surgery, so we don't want to hear any excuses. No more lying around."

"Believe me," I said, tossing the covers aside, "no one wants to be out of this place more than I do. No offense to you and Terri."

"None taken," Terri replied with a grin.

I had no intention of complaining, but it seemed a gargantuan effort just to swing my legs off the bed and set my feet on the floor. All my muscles felt rubbery.

"It's perfectly normal to feel a bit weak at first," Terri said, "but you'll be fine once you start moving."

"No problem," I said. "I got this."

Nevertheless, it took me a minute or two to take the first step and walk fully upright, and I didn't enjoy having to shuffle down the hall like a senior citizen, but I was determined to get back on my feet so I could be discharged as soon as possible.

"You did great," Nurse Terri said when we returned to my room. "I hope we didn't wear you out too much."

"Nope," I replied as she helped me back onto the bed. "So tell me, Terri. What are the odds of a tasty steak dinner tonight? Maybe some mashed potatoes and gravy? A little red wine would be nice."

She glanced up at me flirtatiously as if I'd just asked her out on a date, when all I was referring to was the supper tray that would be delivered later.

"Odds aren't great," she replied. She covered my legs with the blanket.

Another visitor walked in just then, and I felt a rush of adrenalin as I looked up.

"Hi Josh," she said.

Nurse Terri patted me on the shoulder and turned to go. "I'll leave you two alone."

"Carla…" I replied.

Slowly and cautiously—as if she had no idea what sort of reception she would get from me—Carla approached the bed.

M aybe this was the reason I came back from the great beyond—to feel Carla's lips on mine and see that look in her eyes once more. The look that said *I'm still in love with you.*

"How are you feeling?" she asked, taking hold of my hand over the side of the bedrail.

"Good," I replied. "Better."

She squeezed my hand tighter. "We were so worried about you. I want you to know that I was here every day. Kaleigh made you a card. Did you see it?"

I shook my head, so she went to retrieve it from the windowsill where it stood next to the flowers brought in by the carjacking victim.

Carla handed me the card. It was made of light blue construction paper. On the front it said *Get Well Soon* over an image of a sailboat against a sunset, which Kaleigh must have painted herself.

With great care, I opened it and read the note inside:

Dear Josh,
Please come back to us.
Love Kaleigh

For a long moment I stared at the words, hand-printed in navy blue ink, and wondered what she meant by that. Was she trying to tell me she wanted me back in their lives? Or was she referring to my coma?

When Carla and I began dating, Kaleigh was a somewhat prickly thirteen-year-old, and I never really felt as if she'd welcomed me as a potential stepfather. Whenever I came by to visit, she'd disappear into her room to practice her guitar.

So, what was this? Could I dare to hope that she might feel differently now because of what happened to me? Or that Carla might feel differently?

"This is nice," I said, closing the card and lifting my eyes. "Tell her thank you."

Carla took hold of my hand again, stroked the pad of her thumb over my knuckles. "I couldn't believe it when Marie called and told me what happened to you. Then I saw it on the news, and I just felt…"

Her voice broke. She wasn't able to continue.

"You felt what?" I pressed.

Guilt? Regret?

Love?

Carla shook her head as if to clear it. "I don't know. I just wished our last conversation hadn't ended the way it did. I hate the way we parted, with so much anger."

"I was the angry one. Not you."

"But you had every right to feel that way," she said, "and that's not how I wanted it to be. Over the past few days, I couldn't bear to think about how I walked out on you, just leaving things like that, without working it out."

"There was nothing to work out," I firmly said. "You came to tell me you wanted to be with another man and that wasn't what I wanted to hear. It *still* isn't."

Her eyes fell closed, and she reached for a chair to pull closer to the side of the bed. "I'm so sorry, Josh. If only you knew how hard this has been for me."

All I could do was stare at her.

"It's not that I don't care for you," she continued. "I *do*. You're an amazing man, and that's what made this so difficult. I loved what we had together, but there was just something…" She paused. "Something was missing."

So there it was. She hadn't changed her mind after all.

Her words stirred a new cloud of anger in me. Hadn't we already been through this?

"I don't know what you mean by that exactly," I said, "because there was nothing missing for me. But either way, I'm not in the mood to get dumped again, Carla."

She covered her forehead with a hand and sighed. "Oh, I'm so stupid. I shouldn't have come. I'm sorry."

For a moment I watched her shake her head and knew she was mentally punishing herself. Then I thought about Brooke, my other ex-girlfriend who had cheated on me with my best friend. She was a woman I had not been able to forgive. Now here sat Carla who left me for another man she believed was her soul mate—a man who gave her something I couldn't.

Something mystifying. Something she couldn't explain.

This frustrated me to no end.

"There's no need to apologize," I said nonetheless. "I appreciate you coming. It means a lot."

Her watery eyes lifted. "If only you knew how much we prayed for you. Constantly. We didn't want you to die."

I let my head fall back against the pillow and stared up at the ceiling. "Thanks. That's something."

But when I thought about the place I had visited when I flat-lined—how peaceful I felt there, especially in the memories... sitting in the rocking chair as a boy, holding the baby, looking up at Leah—I wasn't convinced all those prayers had done me any favors.

Why in the world *had* I come back? I don't recall making that decision. At least not consciously. Someone must have hit me over the head with a frying pan and pushed me.

Part of me wanted to go back there...to that incredible feeling of perfection. It seemed as if everything was about to become clear to me in that moment when Leah smiled at me, just before I felt the massive jolt.

I was suddenly wracked with confusion and turned my head on the pillow to meet Carla's gaze. "Are you sure about him?" I asked, referring to Aaron Cameron, the man she had chosen over me. "Is there any hope for us?"

Our eyes locked and held.

She shook her head.

My stomach turned over. All I could do was lie there and stare at her.

Eventually, I let out a deep breath. "I'm glad you came," I said in a low voice, "and I hold no ill will. But it's time for you to go now."

Nothing happened for a moment. Then she rose from the chair. Her lips touched my cheek. I closed my eyes, savoring the sensation, imprinting it in my mind forever.

"I'm so glad you're all right," Carla whispered in my ear.

I simply nodded and watched her leave.

Seventeen

My visit with Carla took a lot out of me. After she left, I didn't have the energy to talk to my family. All I wanted to do was be alone, close my eyes, rest quietly. Accept what was final and could not be changed.

My sister Marie understood. She said she would return with my nieces and nephews that evening.

I'm not sure how long I slept. All I know is that when I woke, a golden light from the setting sun was beaming through the window.

I felt groggy and uncomfortable.

I pressed the call button and waited impatiently. An ambulance siren wailed outside.

Finally, Nurse Becky hurried through the door. "Is everything all right?"

I inched upward on the pillows and grimaced at the stiffness in my body. "I'd like to take another walk."

"Sure. That's a great idea." She approached the bed and lowered the rail. "And very ambitious of you. Most patients have to be dragged kicking and screaming out of their beds after surgery."

"I don't want to just lie around," I told her. "I need to get back to work. Sooner would be better than later."

She hooked her arm under my elbow as I swung my legs over the edge of the bed. "You must really enjoy your job."

Even after getting shot? I asked myself. Was I crazy to want to get back on the street? What would happen the next time I pulled someone over in the rain? Would I even be able to get out of the car?

"I guess so."

Again, my muscles felt weak and rubbery, but I was determined to be mobile again. I couldn't let myself fall into a rut, or God forbid, mope around like a heartsick loser for six weeks.

"You're scheduled for physio tomorrow," Nurse Becky told me as we shuffled toward the door. "And you're doing great. Just remember, even a healthy person would find it a challenge to walk after being asleep for five days."

I wasn't really in the mood for conversation, but I wanted to use my body and I knew I needed someone at my side. At least for today.

We walked the full length of the hall and back, and I realized quickly that that was more than enough. "Thanks, Becky," I said. "I needed that." By then I was feeling a bit dizzy and needed to get back in the bed.

A few minutes later, as I stared up at the white ceiling again, I found myself contemplating the mysteries of the universe—which was not like me at all. But I couldn't figure out why I hadn't felt any fear or anxiety while I hovered over my body in the operating room. I'd known I was dying, yet I felt no regret or sorrow over what I was leaving behind.

It wasn't what I'd expected.

None of it was, considering I was never the type to believe in souls and heaven and all that silly spiritual mumbo jumbo.

A voice in the room startled me out of my thoughts and caused me to jump. "Did someone order a psych consult?"

I lifted my head on the pillow. There stood Leah at the foot of my bed, wearing a white lab coat with a blue shirt underneath it. The evening sunlight from the window reflected blindingly off the aluminum clipboard she hugged to her chest.

"That's a definite yes," I replied, more than a little relieved to see her again, "for the crazy cop in room 604."

Her face lit up with a smile as she moved to the side of my bed.

⋅ɕⲟ⳽⳾⋅

"Let's get you sitting up so I can do a proper assessment," Leah said. She laid the clipboard on the side table and raised the head of my bed with the push of a button. This allowed me an opportunity to admire, up close, the lovely details of her face—and how much she had changed. She sure wasn't a kid anymore.

"Isn't there some sort of conflict of interest here?" I asked. "Because we know each other personally?"

"I didn't mention that to anyone," she said. "Did you?"

"Not a single soul."

"Then let's keep it that way, as long as you promise to be honest with me."

I raised a hand. "Scout's honor, Doctor."

She sat down, reached for the clipboard and pulled a retractable pen out of her breast pocket which she clicked with her thumb. "You were never a Scout, were you, Josh?"

She quickly scribbled something down.

"Looks like you caught me in a lie already. Are you making a note of that in my chart?"

She chuckled. "Relax. I'm just jotting down the time of our interview."

"Is that what they're calling it these days? An interview?"

I waited while she wrote a few more things down, sat forward and crossed her legs.

"I'm just going to ask you a few standard questions to get us started. Are you ready?"

"Fire away."

Pen in hand, she looked down at the chart. "Do you have any medical problems?" Her eyes lifted and she winked at me. "Besides having been shot twice in the past week."

I inched upwards on the bed. "Well, I have no spleen, but otherwise, I'm pretty healthy. I exercise regularly, eat well. My blood pressure's always good."

"Have you ever been diagnosed with a mental illness in the past?"

"No."

"Have you ever seen a mental health provider such as a psychiatrist, psychologist, or social worker before? Perhaps at work?"

Again, I said no, and she asked if I was on any medications, or if anyone in my family suffered from mental illness.

"Not that I know of."

"The next bit relates to your social history," she said. First she asked about my relationships with members of my family and if I'd ever been abused, physically or emotionally.

"No," I said. "And I'm very close to everyone in my family."

"Do you belong to any particular religion?"

"Not really," I replied. "I mean...I was baptized in the Anglican Church, but we only ever went to services on special holidays like Christmas and Easter. It's not really a big part of my life."

She wrote that down as well. "Would you describe yourself as a chronic worrier?"

"No."

"Have there ever been extended periods of time where you felt down? No energy? Trouble sleeping? Not just for a week or two, but for many weeks, perhaps months?"

I thought about all the nights I'd tossed and turned when I was thinking about Carla. "I've had some trouble sleeping lately, but I don't think it qualifies."

"Why not?"

"Because it was normal, everyday relationship stuff. Things were going downhill with my girlfriend. Then she dumped me."

"I'm sorry to hear that," Leah replied. "When did this happen?"

Suddenly I wished I'd kept my big mouth shut and had simply answered no to the question.

"The morning I was shot," I told her. "Clearly it was one of those days I should have just stayed in bed."

Leah's eyebrows pulled together with concern. "How long were you seeing this woman?"

"About a year."

"So it was serious, then." She wrote something else down.

"I suppose you could say that," I replied, "considering I'd just bought her an engagement ring." I shrugged a shoulder. "But what are you gonna do, right? She fell for some other guy she thought was her one true love, so I had to withdraw from the race."

Leah stared at me. "Interesting that you would use the word 'race.' Do you consider yourself a competitive person?"

"Definitely."

"And how did you feel about coming in second with this woman?"

I shrugged again. "That's life, right? All's fair in love and war?"

She watched my expression a little too closely. I felt grossly exposed and soon found myself averting my gaze.

"Anything else you want to say about that?" Leah asked. "We could set up a time to talk about it some more if you like."

I shook my head. "No."

She wrote some more things down. Then she flipped the page, paused a moment and took a breath.

"All right then. We'll leave it at that for now. What about hallucinations, Josh? Have you ever had any unusual experiences such as hearing voices that other people can't hear? Or seeing things other people can't see? Or do you have unusual ideas, such as feeling that you have special powers that no one else has?"

I hesitated a moment, and she watched me intently.

"It's written in my chart, I suppose?" I asked. "That's why you're asking this question?" Great. Now I sounded paranoid.

She continued to stare at me. "What's written in your chart?"

"What I told Dr. Crosby when I first woke up last night. That I might have had a..." I paused again.

"You might have had a *what*, Josh?"

I cleared my throat. "It'll probably sound ridiculous, but I think I might have had a..." I lowered my voice even further. "A near-death experience during surgery."

When she did nothing but blink at me, I quickly raised a hand. "Look, if it's all the same to you, I don't want that to go on my record at work. That's the last thing I need because they don't typically issue a weapon to a cop who's delusional or being diagnosed with some sort of weird psychosis."

Again, Leah simply watched me, and I sensed she was waiting for me to elaborate on what happened. Or what I *thought* happened.

When I didn't offer anything more, she clicked the finial on the top of her ballpoint pen and slipped it into her breast pocket.

"Was it an out-of-body experience?" she asked.

I wet my lips. "I don't know. Maybe I went to heaven for a minute, except that I don't really believe in that stuff. I was hoping…maybe *you'd* know, being a psychiatrist and everything. Have you ever dealt with anyone who's experienced something like this before? Is it common?"

Leah reclined back in her chair. "I wouldn't say it's common, but it's not unheard of either. Personally I haven't dealt with it as a clinician and I'll be honest with you, Josh: Most members of the medical community are skeptical about near-death experiences. Based on the literature I've read, it's usually documented that the patient experienced something—in most cases some sort of hallucination. But there are those out there who are interested in finding answers. I'm sure they'd love to talk to you as part of their research."

"I don't want to be anyone's lab rat," I told her. "I'm only sharing this with you because I trust you and I want to figure out what happened."

Leah sat forward and rested her elbow on her knee, her chin on her fist. "What do *you* think happened?"

I stared at her uneasily. "I'm pretty sure I died during the surgery and somehow I witnessed what was happening in the OR from a place outside my body. I just want to understand how that could happen. And what was the light I saw? Was it God? Or is that what happens when the brain shuts down? Is it physiological?"

Lean leaned back and rested her temple on her forefinger. "Most researchers don't consider it proof of God or heaven or the afterlife, although some are trying to prove there's a connection.

On the upside, there's a lot of interest in the subject and studies are being done all the time."

"What do *you* believe?" I asked.

She let out a sigh. "First of all, it doesn't really matter what I believe, because we all have our own unique set of spiritual beliefs. But if you want my honest opinion as a medical professional, I think this is something beyond our ability to understand at this point in time. Maybe someday we'll be able to prove what it is, but for now, it's still considered fringe science. With that said, I have an open mind."

A profound sense of relief moved through me. "So you don't think I'm crazy?"

She chuckled softly. "That's not a word I like to use when I'm describing my patients."

I felt the corner of my mouth curl up in a grin. "Sorry."

"Apology accepted, but on one condition—if you'll tell me more about your experience."

I glanced at the chart she'd set aside. "Can it be off the record?"

"I can't promise you that," she replied, "but for now I'll stop taking notes if it makes you feel more comfortable. I'll just listen, because I'm curious to hear what you remember about that night—specifically, what happened when you flat-lined. Then I'll do some research and see if I can find you some answers."

"That would be helpful," I said.

Just then, we heard the squeaky wheels of the meal cart in the hall. My stomach growled rowdily.

"That must be the juicy steak I ordered," I said.

Leah checked her watch and reached for her clipboard. "Wow. I can't believe how long I've been in here. Time just flew. I have some other things I need to do but I'm on the night shift if you'd like to continue this later?"

"Sure," I replied. "My sister Marie is coming by later. I'm sure she'd love to see you."

Leah stood up. "Marie? I'd love to see her, too. How is she doing these days?"

"She's great. She married a really good guy. He works for the city and they have three adorable kids."

Leah started to go. "That's wonderful. I'll try to come by. I'll see you later, all right?"

With that, she left the room.

The very next second, the orderly walked in. "Look what I have for you. Chicken with potatoes and carrots."

It wasn't exactly the big juicy steak I'd been dreaming about—and sadly there was no wine with the meal—but my mouth watered like Niagara Falls when he lifted the stainless steel lid and I breathed in the delectable scent of solid food. At last.

❧

Leah didn't return until shortly after 9:00 p.m., and she began
apologizing as soon as she entered the room. "I'm so sorry,
Josh. There was a suicide case in the ER and I had to admit
someone. Did Marie come?"

"Yeah. I told her you worked here and she was really hoping
to see you."

"I wanted to see her, too. Maybe tomorrow if she visits?" Leah
approached the bed. "And I know it's late. If you're too tired, we
can reschedule this. I just didn't want you to wait up for me."

"We don't need to reschedule," I said. "If you're free now, I
can talk. It's either you or something boring on television."

She moved closer and sat down on the chair beside the bed.
"All right. I can't promise to be very exciting, though."

"Me neither."

She reached into her pocket for her pen. "But as soon as you
start yawning, I'm calling it a day."

"Deal," I replied.

❧

Because I trusted Leah, I was willing to describe every detail of
my experience in the operating room, and how I floated to the

ceiling and moved toward a light that drew me in and escorted me to another luminous place.

"It's true what they say about your life flashing before your eyes," I told her. "I saw everything. I felt it, as if it were happening in real time, yet a part of me knew it wasn't. I knew I'd been shot and that my body was dying, yet I was reliving the past. The last memory I had was from the day I met you, Riley, and your mom in the hospital when your sister was born. It was Christmas. Do you remember that?"

Leah nodded.

"Strangely, I think it was your voice that pulled me out of that memory and helped me regain consciousness. Or maybe that's why I was having that memory in the first place—because you were here and talking to me. Which came first? The chicken or the egg? Anyway, the next thing I knew, I was staring up at your penlight, here in this room."

Leah pushed a lock of hair behind her ear and sat forward. "Tell me more about those beings of light. You mentioned that you recognized your grandmother? Did she speak to you?"

"There weren't really any actual words spoken," I explained, "but I knew she was saying hello and welcoming me. There were others that seemed familiar, but I couldn't make out who they were. It was a bit fuzzy."

"Fuzzy," she repeated.

I nodded. "I was...*disoriented*. I was resisting everything I was seeing. Like I didn't want to believe it was real."

"Were you afraid?"

"Not at all." I looked down at my hands on my lap. "It seems odd to me now, how people fear death."

"How do you feel about being back among the living?" she asked. "Any regrets?"

I had to think about that for a moment. I hadn't enjoyed coming back just to get dumped a second time by the woman I loved.

"I don't know yet," I said. "Part of me is wondering if I returned for a specific purpose. I kind of feel like I was pushed."

"Pushed? By whom?"

I shrugged. "I don't know. Maybe that's crazy. Maybe all of this is crazy. But I feel like that ball of light knew something I didn't. It struck me as being very knowledgeable."

Leah wrote that down.

"I can't believe I'm telling you this," I said. "If you were any other doctor, I doubt I would say a word. I don't want this to affect my job."

Then came the inevitable yawn.

Leah flipped the chart closed. "It's time for you to get some sleep. We can continue this tomorrow. There are some other things I'd like to talk to you about as well, if you're up to it."

"You know where I am," I said, "although I think I'm scheduled for some physio during the day."

"That's all right. I'm on the night shift again anyway. Sleep well." Leah bent forward and kissed me on the forehead. "And for the record," she added, her face mere inches from mine, "I don't usually make a habit of kissing my patients goodnight at the end of an interview, but this is different."

"Because we're old friends," I replied, feeling a spark of awareness in my veins from the warmth of her touch.

She stroked her hand across my forehead and spoke in a whisper. "Yes. I'm glad you're all right. I'll see you tomorrow?"

I nodded and watched her go.

After she was gone, the room seemed extraordinarily empty.

Twenty

⸎

The following day, I spent an hour in the physiotherapy department where I exercised my muscles and was taught movements I could do on my own while lying in bed. Afterward, I returned to my room to find my partner, Scott, waiting there.

"Hey, you look great," he said optimistically, setting aside the magazine he was reading. He rose to his feet. "It's good to see you."

"You, too," I replied before limping back to the bed.

The nurse lowered the side rail and helped me onto the mattress, while I silently braved the pain in my leg after that challenging hour of stretching and moving.

She covered me with the sheet and chatted with Scott for a minute before leaving us alone.

"How's your arm?" I asked him.

"Fine," he replied, bending and flexing it. "All they did was bandage me up and send me on my way. You're the one who took a beating that night. But we got the guy, thanks to you. He'll be doing time, no doubt about that."

"That's good news. Are you back at work yet?"

Scott sat down in the chair and rolled up the magazine which he held on his lap. "No. They gave me a week off to recover. When I go back they're saying they'll want to keep me in the station for a few weeks. I suspect they'll be sending me out for some therapy, just to make sure I'm not going to freeze up the next time I pull someone over on the turnpike. You should expect the same when you get back."

I nodded with understanding. "I'm already talking to someone. They ordered a psych consult about thirty seconds after I opened my eyes."

"No kidding? The stuff we have to put up with..." He shook his head. "Otherwise, are you doing okay? I heard from some of the guys...it was rough that night. They weren't sure if you were going to make it."

"I almost didn't."

He squeezed the rolled up magazine in his hands and tapped it on his palm. "You're some lucky."

"Tell me about it."

Neither of us said anything for an awkward minute or two.

"I was talking to Marie on the phone," Scott said out of the blue. "She told me Carla came in to see you a bunch of times. She must have felt pretty guilty about the whole thing."

It seemed everyone wanted to talk about Carla. Everyone but me.

"Yeah, she came by yesterday, but I told her not to worry about anything. We're done now and I told her what happened wasn't her fault."

"You're really done?" Scott asked. "Did you tell her about the ring?"

"God, no," I practically barked. "And I'm glad she walked out on me before I made *that* mistake. Her timing was impeccable, actually. Now I just need to put it behind me and move on because she was right. It wasn't meant to be. And if I could survive two bullets, I'm sure I'll survive this, too. It's not like I haven't been dumped before."

Though it still stung. And I still wanted a family. I wanted kids. I just wished I hadn't been so sure Carla was the one. It made me question my judgement.

"That's the spirit," Scott said. "Now we just have to get you out of here and back into the old routine."

"Sure."

Besides all that, there had to have been a reason I was pushed back into this life. I was determined to find out what that reason was—and to do that, I had to get on with the business of living.

Cognition

I am constantly amazed by the resilience of the human body, and more importantly the human spirit. Three days after waking from a five-day coma as a result of two gunshot wounds and major surgery, I was walking steadily—albeit slowly—on a treadmill.

At this rate, the doctors told me it wouldn't be long before I would be discharged. Surprisingly, I had mixed feelings about that.

"Every time you come to see me," I said to Leah one evening after visiting hours were over, "you ask questions about my life and how I feel about this or that. I answer your questions and you scribble things down in my chart. Then you run off because you have some other patient to see. Is it possible that we could have a conversation where you're not talking to me as a patient? Could you just be Leah, the girl I knew when we were kids?"

Her expression warmed. She checked her watch and laid her clipboard down on the windowsill. "I suppose I'm due for a break. What would you like to talk about?"

To my great pleasure, she moved away from the window, shrugged out of her lab coat and folded it over the foot of my bed. I couldn't help but notice the slender curve of her hips in that tight-fitting, blue cotton T-shirt and navy cargo pants.

Reaching for the gel pen on the bedside table, I clicked it a few times with my thumb to tease her. "Just to warn you, I might need to take some notes."

Leah laughed and moved a little closer. She sat on the chair beside me. "I deserve that."

"Yes, you do." Leaning toward her, I reached out. "Give me your hand."

"What for?" she asked with a playful glimmer in her eye.

"You'll see."

She turned her hand over so I could look at her palm. I wanted to trace all the graceful lines with my forefinger and draw a path up to the delicate blue veins at her wrist, but I resisted the urge and instead wrote some numbers up the inside of her arm.

"What's this?" she asked.

"My cell number," I replied, lounging back on the pillows and setting the pen back on the table. "When I get out of here—which should be in the next few days—I don't want to lose touch with you like I did the last time. I'm hoping you'll call."

She rubbed her thumb over my phone number, and smiled. "They'll think I got a tattoo."

"Who's they?" I asked.

"Everyone," she replied after a pause. "The nurses. Other doctors. Patients."

It was not lost on me that she didn't mention her parents, friends, or a significant other, which made me wonder about her personal life. Or lack of one.

"Who cares what anyone thinks?" I asked. "Just promise me you'll call."

Her green eyes lifted, and I wanted to stay there forever in the way she looked at me.

"I promise we won't lose touch this time," she said.

Maybe I was a fool, but I totally believed her.

"Tell me about your family," I said. "How are your parents? What's Riley been up to?"

Leah perched an elbow on the armrest of the chair. "My parents, surprisingly, are still together, which I consider a miracle, because you must remember what my father was like."

"Yes, sir—sergeant major general," I gently replied.

Leah chuckled.

"What was it like for you after you moved out of our old neighborhood?" I asked. "You went to private school, didn't you?"

"Yes, and I learned to play the clarinet. Daily lessons and a front row position in the school band."

"Do you still play?" I asked.

She inclined her head. "Sadly, no. The truth is I sucked. I made the cats howl."

I laughed. "What about Riley? Where is he now?"

Leah gazed at me lingeringly. "You don't know?"

"No. We lost touch, remember?"

Another siren wailed from somewhere outside the hospital, and Leah regarded me with a look of sorrow. "I thought you might have heard about it because you're a police officer."

That got my attention. "Heard about what?"

She raked her fingers through her hair. "It's not easy to talk about because we had a rough time as a family." She paused.

"When Riley was in his early twenties, he was convicted of drug trafficking, breaking and entering, and some other offenses. He spent five years in prison." She paused. "You look surprised."

"I am," I replied. "I had no idea. It must have been before I joined the force. How did it happen? And *when* did it happen?"

She gazed off into space. "I guess it all started when he was in high school. He fell in with a bad crowd, smoked a lot of weed, stayed out late or didn't come home at all. He and Dad fought constantly—it was like a war zone in our house most of the time. There was a lot of shouting and doors slamming and hitting and smacking. As soon as Riley turned eighteen, he moved out, and Dad told him not to come back. Ever."

"That does sound rough," I agreed.

"We didn't hear from him for about two years, which was really hard on Mom. We had no idea where he was. Then he broke into our house one night with a couple of small-time drug dealers to steal whatever they could. Dad went downstairs with a baseball bat, and poor Holly was terrified. She and my mother had to lock themselves in the bathroom."

"Holly?" I asked, interrupting.

"My baby sister," Leah explained.

"Oh. I didn't know that was her name. It makes sense, since she was born on Christmas."

Leah nodded again. "Anyway, Mom called 911 that night, not knowing that it was her own son who had smashed our back window and broken into the house. Before the cops arrived, Dad hit Riley with the bat. Practically split his head open. There was blood all over the floor. He said it was dark and he didn't know that it was Riley."

"Did you believe him?"

"I don't know," she quietly replied.

"What happened after that?" I had to ask.

"Riley and his friends took off when they heard the sirens, but the cops caught them hiding in a shed down the street."

"Was Riley okay?" I asked.

"He had a concussion but it wasn't serious. He pleaded guilty in court."

All of it was difficult to hear and I couldn't help but wonder how their lives might have turned out if they'd never moved out of our neighborhood. Would things have been different?

"He must be out of prison by now," I said, hungering for more information.

"He is," Leah explained, "but while he was in there, Dad forbade any of us from visiting. I know for a fact that Mom went secretly, at least for the first couple of years, but she said prison changed Riley to the point that she didn't even recognize him anymore. The last we'd heard, he drove out west with some ex-cons he met in jail. For all I know, he could be dead from an overdose by now." She shut her eyes and rubbed her hands over her face. "I'm sorry. It hurts to talk about it."

I gave her a moment to regain her composure.

"If you like, I could try and locate him for you," I carefully offered.

She thought about that. "Thank you, Josh, but the truth is—and it shames me to admit this—I'm not even sure I want to know, because what if it's bad news?" She gazed out the window. "God help us all if it is. None of us even *tried* to find him. For some reason, we all just stuck our heads in the sand. It's probably my biggest regret in life—that I didn't try harder to do something before things got so out of control."

"It wasn't your fault," I told her. "You were young. You couldn't have known how things would turn out. As far as I'm concerned, you were a great sister."

Her gaze met mine. "Was I? All I remember is wanting to please Dad, and being more preoccupied with what *he* wanted than worrying about what my younger brother was getting into. I wanted to get the highest grades, the biggest scholarship, get accepted into med school. Meanwhile, Riley just rebelled."

As I listened to her talk, I felt suddenly out of my depth.

"But you've done well for yourself," I finally said. "You should be proud of what you've accomplished."

Leah looked down at the floor. "Thanks. You know…I think a part of me chose this specialty because of Riley. I always wished I'd had the skills to help him. But it's too late for that now."

"It's never too late to help someone," I reminded her.

"Mmm."

She rested her temple on a finger and gazed at me thoughtfully with those deep green eyes that made me feel like I was floating down a lazy river. They were so achingly familiar. It was like going home.

"I'm sure Riley would love that," she said with a note of sarcasm. "His big sister psychoanalyzing him." She let out a resigned sigh. "The truth is, I think he resented me for setting the bar so high and I've always felt guilty about that."

I stared at her, openmouthed, because I'd never had such a frank discussion with a woman before. I was reminded of the moment I floated upwards and looked down at my body, bleeding on the operating table. Now I was looking at Leah, and she was holding a surgical instrument in her hand…the knife she had just used to open her own heart before my eyes.

"I'll look him up for you," I said with firm resolve. "You never know. Maybe he's turned his life around."

She thought about it for a long time. "Maybe you're right. Would you mind doing that for us?"

"Of course not. I want to."

Leah checked her watch and stood up. "Look at that. I have to go." She moved to put her lab coat back on.

"We didn't accomplish much tonight," I casually mentioned as I watched her check her pockets and fetch her clipboard from the windowsill. "You didn't write a single word in my chart."

"I was on a break, remember?" she replied with an easy smile. "Listen, I'm off tomorrow so I won't see you, but I want to say something. When you go back to work, they'll likely be on the lookout for signs of PTSD."

"You mean post-traumatic stress disorder," I said.

"That's right," she replied. "Watch for symptoms, okay? You might feel fine now, but when you get back in the squad car, you may experience some anxiety, or you might have nightmares about the shooting. I wanted to talk to you about that, but I'm not sure we'll get the chance if they discharge you. Just remember that it's very common and there are ways to deal with it, so accept help if the department offers it. Don't worry about that, okay? You'll get through it."

She started for the door.

"Wait...Leah..." I sat forward. "Will you come and see me tomorrow?"

"I told you, I'm off," she replied.

"I know, but you could come by and visit anyway. Leave the lab coat at home. You could smuggle in a grilled steak for me."

She gave me a dazzling smile. It's a wonder I didn't fall out of bed and hit my head on the floor.

"I'll try." Then she tapped a finger on her arm. "But if I don't make it tomorrow and you get discharged, at least I'm tattooed with your phone number."

"But I don't have yours," I quickly replied with a flash of worry because I didn't want to lose touch with her again.

She must have recognized my concern, because she lowered the chart to her side and approached the foot of the bed. "You know where I live, don't you? The big red Victorian on Russell Street? I had to move back in with my parents recently. You should come by, Josh. No need to call first. My mom loves visitors and I know she'd be thrilled to see you."

Relaxing somewhat, I sat back and committed her address to my memory.

"I will," I said. "But maybe I'll try to come by when your father's not at home. Does he work days or nights?"

She chuckled. "That's not necessary. With Riley gone, no one is pushing his buttons anymore. I'm sure he'd love to see you."

"All right then."

She seemed in a hurry to leave suddenly.

As she backed away, I felt a strong urge to reach out and hold on to her. Yet something in me feared she would slip through my grasp if I tried. That she'd disappear like a fine cool mist. Just like all the other women in my life.

"Come by soon, all right?" she said. "As soon as you're discharged. Promise?"

"I will."

Appearing satisfied, she turned and left the room.

I immediately grabbed the pen on the bedside table and scribbled the address on the back of a magazine.

Russell Street. Big red Victorian.

Two days later I was discharged with instructions to return to the hospital for regular physiotherapy appointments over the next four weeks. I was not permitted to return to work for at least six weeks.

That didn't stop me from calling Scott, however, to ask him to do me a favor and dig up information on Riley James. I told him that Riley's last known whereabouts were somewhere on the west coast, but he could be anywhere by now—possibly back in Boston or back in prison again in some other part of the country.

Meanwhile, my sister Marie and my mom came by my apartment often with home cooked meals in plastic containers. My mother begged me repeatedly to come stay with her because she couldn't imagine how I could get up and down the steep stairs of my apartment without assistance.

I assured her that climbing stairs was good for me, but I promised to take it slow.

A full week went by. Leah didn't call.

The following week, however, my cell phone rang while I was in the shower. Normally, I would have let it go to voice mail, but I decided to step out and towel off to answer it.

I'm very glad I did.

⤚ᴄ

There could be no doubt about it. The information I gleaned from that phone call provided a legitimate excuse for me to visit Leah. It was certainly better than just sitting around, waiting for her to call. Knowing that she often worked nights at the hospital, I decided to pop by in the afternoon.

A light rain was falling as I left my apartment, got into my car and started up the engine. The wipers beat steadily across the windshield as I pulled away from the curb and headed across town. As I drove, I pondered how I was going to deliver the information I'd just received about Riley.

Part of me felt torn. It had been twenty-five years since I'd had any contact with this family, so maybe they'd consider me a stranger and ask why I was poking my nose into their personal affairs. They might not even recognize me at the door. Maybe Leah was right. Maybe they didn't even *want* to know about Riley. That prospect had occurred to me more than once, because surely if Dr. and Mrs. James wanted to know what had become of their son, they could have found a way. At the very least, they could have hired a private investigator.

Maybe they had. Maybe they already knew the truth but chose not to share it with Leah. Maybe they didn't want to open old wounds.

In the end, as I turned up Russell Street in search of their Victorian mansion, all that mattered to me was what Leah wanted. Based on our conversation at the hospital, I sensed in her a desire to bring me into this. It's why she told me everything she did, and why she had given me her address.

The house was perched far back on a grassy rise overlooking the street, and the driveway was large enough to accommodate at least six cars.

I pulled up next to the stone walkway, shut off the engine, and leaned forward over the steering wheel to look up at the front of the house.

It boasted a large, covered veranda with ornamental spindles, a massive front door with a half-moon shaped transom, and bay windows beneath decorative, white cornices.

After dropping my keys into my pocket, I opened the car door and got out. The rain was coming down harder by then, but I knew I couldn't make a run for it on account of my leg, so I drew up the hood of my jacket and limped up the freshly painted blue steps.

Once I made it to the covered veranda, I lowered my hood, shook off the raindrops, and rang the bell. It chimed like an old grandfather clock.

I waited and waited, but no one answered, so I rang the bell a second time and continued to wait.

Just when I was about to turn away, the heavy oak door creaked open. Suddenly I found myself staring through the screen at a somber-looking young woman with golden hair and blue eyes set wide apart.

"Yes?" She looked as if she'd just woken from a nap.

I'm not sure if I was tongue-tied because I'd expected Leah to answer the door, or if I was knocked off kilter because there was something jarringly familiar about this woman and it sent my stomach into a spin.

Was this Holly? The tiny newborn baby I'd held in my arms twenty-five years ago? If so, she was still very petite. She couldn't have been more than five foot two.

"I'm looking for Leah James," I explained. "I'm Josh. Josh Wallace."

The young woman frowned at me. For some reason, I felt a strange compulsion to apologize for my presence.

"Do I have the right house?" I asked.

She blinked a few times. "How do you know Leah?"

I raised my shoulders against the damp chill of the rainstorm and buried my hands in my pockets. "We lived on the same street when we were kids. I was best friends with her brother, Riley. Are you Holly?"

She regarded me with what appeared to be a hint of displeasure, then pushed the screen door wide open. "You should come in."

Stepping inside, I glanced around the wide, cherry-wood panelled entranceway and spacious parlors to the left and right. Every piece of furniture was an antique and the fireplaces were enormous. "You have a beautiful home," I said.

"Thank you." She shut the door and folded her arms to close the long grey sweater she wore.

"So…you must be Holly?" I asked a second time.

"Yes."

An uncomfortable silence ensued and I wondered if I should have made other arrangements to see Leah, because I did not feel the least bit welcome here.

"Actually," I said, gazing down at her in a friendly attempt to turn things around, "you wouldn't remember this, but we met once before. I came to the hospital to visit you on the day you were born. It was Christmas Day."

Holly inclined her head. "That's right. My birthday is December 25th."

"I was only ten," I added, "but I rocked you in a chair. You were the first baby I ever held." I chuckled. "I was afraid I'd drop you on your head or something."

Holly didn't break a smile. She merely gathered her woolly sweater tighter around herself. "Have you kept in touch with Leah all this time? She never mentioned you."

"No," I explained. "Your family moved out of our neighborhood just before you were born. That's when your father bought this house." I glanced toward the stairs. "Is your mom here? I'd love to say hello to her."

I wasn't hopeful, because the house seemed eerily quiet.

Holly spoke in a low, monotone voice. "She and Dad went to the cottage for the weekend."

"What about Leah?" I asked. "Is she around? I was hoping to talk to her about something."

Holly frowned again. "No."

"Do you know when she'll be back?"

Pushing her hair back off her forehead, Holly took a deep breath as if to brace herself for something. "She's not coming back. I'm sorry Josh. You obviously don't know."

I shook my head. "Know what?"

A chill, black tension moved across the floor and swirled around me like a snake.

"Leah died two weeks ago," she said. "The funeral was last Tuesday."

The grandfather clock in the front room began to chime, and I could do nothing but stare at Holly in disbelief.

"That can't be right," I said with a rancor that sharpened my voice. "I spoke to her a week ago. In the hospital."

"What hospital?" Holly asked with a shake of her head.

"Mass General," I replied. "I was taken there after I was shot. I'm a police officer."

My words seemed to freeze in Holly's brain, then slowly, she began to nod. "Oh yes, I recognize you. You were on the news. It was a carjacking, wasn't it?"

"That's right. I had to have two bullets removed in surgery and I was in a coma for five days. When I woke up, Leah was there. She was assigned to my case."

I didn't mention that I'd required a psychiatric consult because it wasn't exactly something I wanted to broadcast to the world with a megaphone.

"That can't be," Holly said, "because Leah's gone and she was sick for a long time before that."

By now my heart was pounding like a sledgehammer. "What do you mean...*sick*...?"

Holly closed her eyes briefly, then opened them. "Let me take your coat."

She reached out her hands. I immediately shrugged out of my rain jacket and handed it to her, then followed her to a back corridor with hooks on the wall.

"Would you like something to drink?" she asked. "A cup of coffee or a glass of water? I think we have some ginger ale."

"I'm fine."

"No, you can't be," she asserted. "You can't be fine, because *I'm* not fine. Not after what you just said to me."

Still not completely believing that Leah was gone, I followed Holly to a large modern kitchen at the back of the house with white cabinets and shiny granite countertops. She opened the stainless steel fridge and pulled out two bottles of beer.

"Would you like a glass?" she asked.

"The bottle's fine."

While she used her sweater under the palm of her hand to twist off both caps and hand the beer to me, I felt like I was awake in some sort of strange dream.

"There has to be a mix up," Holly said, leaning her hip against the center island. "Maybe you dreamed it. Were you medicated?"

"At first, yes," I replied, "but I didn't dream it. She was real."

But how could this be? Leah couldn't possibly be dead. She absolutely couldn't.

"Tell me about her being sick," I said.

Holly took a swig of her beer. "Leah had ALS. She was diagnosed a few years ago when she first started her psychiatry residency."

"ALS," I repeated. "That's Lou Gehrig's Disease?"

She nodded. "It affects the nerve cells in the brain and the spinal cord, and then the brain loses the ability to control muscle movement. Eventually the patient can become totally paralyzed, which is what happened to Leah. She was at home with us for the last few months, but we had to send her to the hospital because of complications when she got pneumonia."

"That's when she died?" I asked, finding it difficult to say the word.

Holly nodded.

"Did she work at Mass General as well?" I asked, still feeling confused by all this.

"No. She was doing her residency at a hospital up in Chicago but she had to quit over a year ago when the disease began to progress. She'd been home with us ever since."

I set down my beer, shut my eyes and cupped my forehead in a hand. "God, I'm so sorry. I'm in shock. I swear I talked to her the day before I was discharged, or maybe I did dream it. I was pretty out of it when I woke up."

I began to feel slightly nauseous as the news settled in.

Leah...Gone...

Neither of us said anything for a moment until I opened my eyes.

"But it couldn't have been a dream," I insisted, "because she told me things—like the fact that she was doing a psychiatry residency. I wouldn't have known that. She said she was in third year. She also told me about your brother, Riley."

Holly stared at me with bewilderment. "What exactly did she tell you?"

"That he went to prison for five years. I swear I didn't know that either, and I know it's true because I had my partner look him up and everything Leah told me checked out."

Holly studied my face for a moment, then cleared her throat and turned away. She moved to the other side of the kitchen, as if to put the center island between us. "Are you sure you didn't talk to her…like a year ago? Maybe you're confused because of what happened to you. You were in a coma, weren't you?"

"I was." I held up a hand. "Please don't worry. I'm not crazy and I'm not here to harm you." Reaching into my back pocket, I withdrew my badge which I always carried, even when I was off duty. I laid it on the granite countertop between us. "There's my badge number if you want to write it down."

She stared at it hesitantly, then met my gaze. "It's all right. You can put that away."

I picked it up and slipped it back into my pocket.

We swigged our beers and regarded each other warily.

"What did she look like?" Holly asked. "Can you describe her for me?"

"Sure. Long brown hair, green eyes, slim, about five-foot-seven. I'd estimate a hundred and twenty pounds."

Holly continued to watch me, then gestured for me to follow her out of the kitchen. "There's a picture of her in the living room. Come and see it."

We moved into a large formal room with dark yellow painted walls, cherry oak wainscoting and columns. Holly crossed to the mantelpiece which displayed at least a dozen framed family photographs.

"Here she is," she said, handing me an 8x10 graduation photo. "This was taken when she finished medical school a few ago."

My stomach clenched and I nodded. "Yes, this is her and there's no way I could have known what she looked like, because I swear I haven't seen her since I was ten." I handed the picture back.

Holly ran her fingers over the glass.

"I'm sorry," I said again. "I'm still in shock."

"Me, too," she replied as she carefully set the photo back on the mantle. "But this still doesn't explain what you saw. Or *think* you saw."

"No," I replied, "and I'm a little freaked out right now."

We moved to the sofa and sat down on opposite ends, facing each other.

"I remember seeing something about the carjacking and the shooting on the news," Holly said, "but we were all pretty distracted because it happened right about the time Leah passed. I believe it might have been the same night."

I told her the date and she confirmed that yes, Leah had passed away on the same night I was brought in by ambulance.

Feeling more than a little anxious, I raked my fingers through my hair. "Leah told me that she was working the night they brought me in and that she recognized me on the gurney. She was the first person I saw when I opened my eyes. She was right there, leaning over me, shining a penlight in my eyes. Then she visited me every night and conducted a series of psychiatric interviews."

"Did anyone else see this person who claimed to be Leah?" Holly asked, and I wondered if she thought there might be a doppelganger out there someone who had stolen her sister's identity. It made more logical sense than the alternative which neither of us dared to acknowledge.

"I'm not sure," I said. "There were always nurses and orderlies coming and going. She'd pass them on her way in and out sometimes."

"I'm going to call the hospital right now and ask," Holly said, pulling out her cell phone and dialing the number, which she obviously had on speed dial.

After waiting a moment to be connected to the psych department, Holly asked if there was a resident doctor on staff named

Leah James. "No? Are you sure? She might have just started in the last week or two." She paused. "Okay. Thank you."

She hung up and set her phone down on the coffee table. "There's no resident at Mass General by that name. So either you dreamed it or someone is pretending to be her, which would really piss me off."

I thought of the movie *Catch Me If You Can*, where the main character masqueraded as pilots, doctors and lawyers—a true story, apparently.

But none of that seemed right. I could have sworn I was talking to the real Leah I'd known as a kid. Even her voice was the same.

"You said she performed a psych consult?" Holly mentioned. "Did she write things down in your chart?"

"Yes."

"Then that would be in the records department at the hospital. If I could take a look at it, I'd recognize her handwriting."

"I could go in today and ask to see it," I suggested. "You could come with me if you want."

She shook her head. "They won't just release it to you. It's against hospital policy. They'll get you to fill out a form and that could take awhile. Did they give you a discharge summary when you left?"

"Yes, I have it at home."

"Did you read it? Did Leah sign her name to it?"

I shook my head. "No."

"Are you sure?"

"Yes, I read over the whole thing but there was no mention of the psychiatric interviews, only the physical stuff and some details about follow-up physio treatments. They said they would send a copy to my regular doctor and I'm supposed to book an appointment with him next week."

Holly nodded as if none of this was a surprise to her.

"I shouldn't suggest this," she said, "but I could get my hands on it if you want me to."

"How would you do that?"

"I'm a medical student," she casually explained. "I'm in my second year at Harvard and I have a badge for Mass General. I've been helping out in the ER this semester."

"You're going to be a doctor, too?" I asked. "Does medicine run in your blood or something?"

She rolled her eyes and shook her head. "I doubt that. What I really think is that Dad always knew how to pull our strings, like a great puppet master. Sometimes I think he made monsters out of all of us."

I wasn't sure I understood what she was referring to, exactly, and I didn't get the chance to ask.

"Never mind." She rose from the sofa. "Do you want to go to the hospital now? Because I really want to know what's going on here."

I stood up as well. "This won't be breaking any rules, will it? I'm a cop. I don't want to get you into any trouble."

"We'll be fine as long as I have your express permission to look at your chart. Do I?"

I hesitated a moment. "Yes."

"Okay then. I'll just go into the records department and say your doctor wants to check on something. They'll see my badge and give me the chart, no problem. I'll take a look, then I'll return it. At least we'll know what we're dealing with. If someone is pretending to be my sister, I'll alert the hospital."

I nodded, but somehow I doubted that would be the case. Every instinct in my body was telling me this was something else entirely. Something that might be just cause for committing me to a psych ward for good.

❝There's probably something else I should tell you," I said to Holly as we pulled out of the driveway.

"Something *else*?" she asked, watching my profile.

"Yeah. If I'm going to let you look at my chart, you might see why they ordered the psych consult in the first place, and it's a bit...It's kind of way out there."

"Way out there," she repeated. "Now you have me curious."

I flicked the blinker and pulled onto the street. My tires hissed noisily through puddles on the pavement.

"It's not something I've told anyone except for Leah," I said, "because I'm not comfortable with anyone at the station hearing about it. I want to get back to work as soon as possible and I don't want anyone to think I'm...well, *delusional*."

"I hate to tell you this," Holly said. "But it's a little late for that. Since the moment you walked into my house, you've been suggesting you had conversations with my sister's ghost. I'm wondering if I'm a bit short on common sense, because maybe I shouldn't have gotten into a car with you."

Not knowing whether she was kidding or not, I slid her a look. "I never said ghost. That's your word, not mine."

"Fine." She held her hands up in surrender. "I just think we should call a spade a spade. That's all. So what is this 'other thing' that's further out there than what you've already told me?"

I gently pressed on the brake as we approached a stop sign, then tried my best to explain.

"When I was in surgery having the bullets removed," I said, "my heart stopped and I flatlined. They had to take steps to resuscitate me, and as that was happening, I think I had one of those..." I paused. "Near-death experiences. Have you heard of them?"

"Of course," she resolutely replied. "Did you see a white light?"

Not sure how she was taking this, I glanced at her again and nodded.

"Yes."

"What else happened?" she asked with curiosity. "Can you describe everything to me?"

Turning left onto a busier street, I increased the wiper speed.

"I felt like I was floating out of my body," I explained, "and I watched the operation from a place near the ceiling. When I woke up later I knew they had removed my spleen because I saw them do it, and the doctor confirmed it."

"So you witnessed things you couldn't have known about in your unconscious state." She waited for me to respond.

"Yes."

"Tell me more about the light. Did you move toward it?"

She seemed genuinely fascinated and I was relieved she wasn't looking at me like I had two heads.

"Yes. Listen, you're not going to tell anyone about this, are you? I'd prefer if you kept it just between us."

She made the form of a cross over her chest. "Scout's honor."

"That's not the sign for Scout's honor," I said, recalling that I'd spoken those exact words to Leah not long ago.

"No, I guess not," she replied with a half-smile. "But I promise I won't tell anyone. Mum's the word. Now go on."

Feeling strangely captivated by her interest in my story, I checked my rearview mirror and changed lanes.

"You know all the stuff you hear about your dead relatives greeting you at the pearly gates?" I asked. "It was kind of like that. I saw my grandmother and a bunch of other people I couldn't really recognize. Then I saw what was sort of like a fast motion movie of my life. It was very bizarre."

Holly turned her body slightly on the seat to face me. "It's more common than you think."

"Is it? How would you know?"

"Because I wrote a paper on it during my final year of undergrad."

"No kidding. What did you study?" I asked.

"Neuroscience at Harvard."

Geez. Was she like...a genius?

I turned to look at her with wonder and felt slightly intimidated, intellectually. "Well, I must say that's convenient. Maybe you're the one person in the world who can actually explain what happened to me."

Holly shrugged apologetically. "Sorry. I wish I could, but I was only in second year at the time and my conclusion was that the jury's still out. There are plenty of religious and scientific theories and I could present them all to you—or just let you read my paper. In the end, I suggested that each of us has to make our own choice and believe what makes the most sense to us. It depends on whether you're a person of religious faith, or a person who needs scientific proof of something tangible." She looked out the window. "It wasn't a terribly scientific paper. I got a B minus. It brought my grade down."

"Sorry to hear that, but that's pretty much what your sister said to me."

At the mention of Leah, Holly faced forward again and fell silent.

I drove up the turnpike ramp and merged onto the center lane. "I'm sorry. That sounded flippant. I didn't mean it to be. I still can't believe she's gone. It doesn't seem real. What seems real is that I was talking to her a week ago and I swear, she wasn't a ghost. She was always clicking her ball point pen and I touched her hand and wrote my phone number on her arm. She was flesh and blood, I'm telling you."

Holly turned her attention to me again and let out a soft chuckle. "Seriously, you wrote your phone number on her arm? Were you trying to pick her up or something?"

I gave a sheepish look and winced. "Maybe I kind of thought we might start something up when I got out."

"And that's why you came by the house today," Holly said, as if to clarify my intentions. "To see her again because you liked her."

I nodded, and decided to leave the news about Riley for another time, because we had enough on our plate for now.

"At least you had good taste," Holly said. "Because she was the most amazing person I ever knew."

As soon as we arrived at the hospital, Holly reached into the back seat for her lab coat. Her badge was pinned to the pocket. I dropped her off at the main door and told her I'd find a place to park and meet her in the cafeteria.

Almost an hour later, while I sat alone at a table staring into my black coffee and thinking about Leah's ALS diagnosis at such a young age, Holly approached and sat down across from me.

"Well?" I said. "Were you able to read the chart?"

She leaned forward, folded her hands on the table and stared at me directly. "Yes."

"And? Was it Leah's handwriting?"

Holly's chest expanded and contracted with a heavy sigh. "No, because there was no record of any psychiatric consultations at all. No notes about any of the interviews you described, and her name was nowhere to be found."

The air wafted out of my lungs and I sat back. "*Great*. Now you must think I'm a total nutcase. Completely delusional." I watched the people in the lineup for the cash and shook my head in disbelief. "Would the psych notes be somewhere else, like in the psych department?"

"No, the only place they'd be is in your chart. In the records department."

She continued to watch me intently.

I sat forward and spoke in a hushed tone. "What about the night I woke up?" I realized I was grasping at straws but I had to grasp at something. "I specifically heard Dr. Crosby order the phych consult. He said it to a nurse. Her name was Gayle. I'm sure she would remember that because she seemed shaken that I knew my spleen had been removed."

Holly raised a finger. "I did see the notation for a consult, but there was a line drawn through it, so someone obviously cancelled it. I'm not sure why. Maybe you could talk to your doctor about that because after the trauma you suffered, you're definitely at risk for PTSD."

I leaned back again. "You think I hallucinated everything."

"I really don't know," she gently said. "All I can say for sure is that there was no sign of Leah in your chart. I'm sorry, Josh."

I rested my elbows on the table, pressed my forehead into the heels of my hands. "She was *there*. I'm sure of it. It couldn't have been a dream."

Holly wrapped a hand around my wrist and lowered my hands to the table. "Did anyone else see her or talk to her? A nurse? Maybe one of your family members who was in the room with you?"

I struggled to remember, then shook my head. "No, it was always just the two of us alone, talking. I asked her to come by and see my sister and mother, and she said she would try, but she never did."

Now I was beginning to wonder if I really was losing my mind.

But that wouldn't explain all the things Leah had told me about her brother Riley and how it checked out when Scott looked into it. I hadn't brought any of that up with Holly yet, but I sure as hell intended to.

But first...

"I need to talk to Dr. Crosby," I said, rising from my chair. "I want to ask him why he cancelled the psych order."

"Would you mind if I came with you?" Holly asked.

"You've come this far," I replied. "You might as well stick around for the rest." I gestured with a hand for her to follow.

"For some reason," I said to Dr. Crosby when I found him walking briskly down the corridor outside the ICU, "when I got up this morning, I remembered that you had ordered a psychiatric consult when I woke up from my coma. Do you remember that?"

I glanced over at Holly who was waiting discreetly by the elevators.

"Yes," he replied, and stopped to face me. "But now that you mention it, I don't recall seeing any notes on that," he said. "Did someone come and see you?"

"No," I answered. "I thought maybe you'd cancelled it."

He stared at me for a moment, then frowned. "I apologize, Josh. I wasn't the one who followed up on your case because Dr. York took over for me. I don't know how that could have slipped through the cracks. You should definitely have talked to someone. I can set that up for you now, if you'd like."

I shook my head. "No, it's not really necessary because I'll be seeing someone through work." I wasn't absolutely certain about that, but I assumed it would be the case.

Dr. Crosby regarded me intently. "Have you had any other experiences like what you described to me when you first regained consciousness?"

I looked down at my shoes. "No, and I'm kind of embarrassed about that. I think it was a dream, like you said. I was pretty out of it. I feel better now."

"Good to hear." He nodded reluctantly. "All right then. Just make sure you follow up with your regular physician in a week or two."

"I will. Thank you."

I met Holly's gaze from across the distance, and shrugged. Then I waved for her to follow me again, because I wanted to see if I could find Nurse Gayle. Maybe *she* was the one who had cancelled the order, either by mistake or under the instructions of Dr. York.

"So it wasn't Nurse Gayle or Dr. York who cancelled the order," Holly said as we got into my car. The rain had finally let up and the sun was peeking out from behind a cloud. "It won't be easy to find out who cancelled it. You'd have to confront everyone who worked those shifts when you were in recovery because it was just a line drawn through the order in regular blue pen. No one initialed it or anything."

"Maybe I was dreaming the whole thing with Leah," I said as I inserted the key into the ignition and started the engine. "And maybe I need professional help."

"I'm not suggesting that," she said, somewhat defensively.

"No, but you're thinking it and I can't blame you. What I'm telling you is crazy. It's *beyond* crazy."

I slung my arm over the back of Holly's seat to look out the rear window as I reversed the car out of the parking spot. A few minutes later, we were back on the turnpike, moving at a steady clip with the rest of the traffic.

"I still can't believe she's gone," I softly said as I stared blankly at the car in front of us. "And that she died on the same day I arrived at the hospital. Don't you think that's strange?"

"I do," Holly replied in a solemn tone. She sat quietly until we merged onto the exit that led into her neighborhood. "God, something just occurred to me—something I read in your chart."

I turned to glance at her while still keeping most of my attention on the road. "What was it?"

"I skimmed over everything, Josh, but what's almost too coincidental to ignore is the fact that you were brought in by ambulance and admitted to the ER at the exact hour of Leah's death. She may not have worked at Mass General, but that's where she died."

I pulled to a stop at the bottom of the ramp. "What are you suggesting?"

Holly regarded me soberly. "That maybe she was having an out of body experience as well. Except that—unlike you—she never returned to her body."

Twenty-nine

I pulled into Holly's driveway, parked the car and turned off the engine.

"In some cases I studied," she said as she got out of the car and shut the door, "patients described floating out of the room they were in, moving through walls and seeing other things that were happening in the hospital. Maybe that's what happened to Leah. Maybe she saw you enter the ER, recognized you and wanted to stick around to make sure you were okay."

"Now *you're* sounding crazy," I said, as I stepped out of the car as well. I shut the door and pressed the lock button on my key ring. The vehicle beeped.

Following Holly up the front walk—while trying to ignore the throbbing ache in my thigh after walking too quickly around the hospital—I could barely fathom what we were discussing. This just wasn't the kind of thing I had ever been into, except for being a fan of movies like *Poltergeist* or *Amityville Horror*.

We climbed the steps and she unlocked the front door. We entered and she set her purse on the small mahogany table by the stairs.

"I hope you don't have plans for tonight," she said, "because I'd love it if you could stay for supper. Clearly there's a lot to talk about and I'm all alone here anyway. At least for tonight." There was a melancholy look in her eye, and I knew she was missing Leah.

"I don't have plans," I said.

"Good. Are you hungry now? And are you okay with left-overs? I made a lasagne last night and hardly ate any of it."

"I love lasagne," I replied.

"Great." She pointed a finger. "You can hang your coat up in the back hall, then come on into the kitchen and have a seat." She glanced down at my leg briefly before leaving me.

I shrugged out of my jacket and hung it up, then bent over for a minute to take a few deep breaths. My leg was stiff and throbbing and my abdomen was sore. I'd definitely done too much walking.

A moment later, I found Holly uncorking a bottle of red wine on the center island and pouring two glasses. Maybe that would help numb the pain, I thought as I approached and slid up onto a stool.

She opened the fridge and withdrew a pan of lasagna wrapped in foil which she carried to the stovetop.

"How thoughtless of me," she mentioned as she pressed the power buttons on the oven. "I didn't even ask if you liked red wine before I poured it. I have beer if you'd prefer that."

"Wine is good," I replied, reaching for the stemmed glass she had placed in front of me.

She opened the oven door, slid the lasagne inside and set the timer for half an hour. "Are you okay?" she asked, glancing at my leg again. "Is that bothering you?"

"I'm fine. It just aches sometimes when I overdo it."

"Stay seated, then," she said. "I'll make us a salad. We can talk while I chop."

Holly returned to the fridge and withdrew some lettuce, car-rots, cucumbers and tomatoes from the vegetable drawer. She set everything on the island and slid a blade out of the stainless steel knife block.

"How long were you in a coma?" she asked as she washed the lettuce at the sink.

"Five days—and this part you might find interesting. Remember when I told you that I watched my life flash before my eyes?"

"Like a fast motion movie?" she mentioned.

"Yes. Well...get this. The moment I was reliving, just before I woke up, was the day I visited you in the hospital when you were born. Leah was the one who put you in my arms as I sat in a rocking chair. Then she started saying things like, 'Open your eyes, Josh. Can you hear me?' I was confused because I was living in that memory, but when I opened my eyes, there she was."

"What do you think it means?" Holly asked, watching me with interest. I still wasn't sure if she thought I was insane and was just testing me or humoring me, or if she believed there was something real about all this. "Do you think there was some sort of overlap between your memories and your return to the real world?"

"Maybe."

I then recounted everything I could remember about my conversation with Leah that first night. I also told Holly about the questions she'd asked when she returned the next day to conduct the first interview.

"She seemed to do everything by the book," I said, "ticking off boxes, asking standard questions. She seemed very competent. It never—not even for a single second—occurred to me that she might not be a genuine doctor."

"Oh, she was genuine," Holly said. "When it comes to medicine and psychiatry, she was brilliant. She graduated at the top of her class and if she hadn't gotten sick, I'm sure she'd be working somewhere amazing right now, making an incredible difference in people's lives."

"What about you?" I asked. "You must have done pretty well for yourself, to get accepted to the neuroscience program at Harvard. Then med school. Were you always a good student?"

She shrugged indifferently as she tore the lettuce leaves off the stalks and tossed them into the salad bowl. "I don't know that I was any smarter than anyone else. I just worked really hard. You wouldn't believe how strict my dad was about homework and extra-curricular activities."

"I do believe it," I replied, sensing some obvious bitterness. "Remember, I lived down the street from Leah and Riley, so I knew your father. I still feel guilty about the fact that your family moved out of our neighborhood. For a long time, I blamed myself for that."

"Why?" She tossed more lettuce into the bowl.

I went on to tell her the story of Riley and me biking to the old Clipper Lake Hotel and getting locked in the stairwell.

"That was the night your father warned me to stay away. A For Sale sign went up the following week, and it was the end of our friendship as we knew it."

"I can't say I'm surprised," Holly said with a shake of her head. "But I'm sure there were other reasons why my dad wanted to move. I saw pictures of that house. I suspect it wasn't quite good enough for his lavish tastes. It was probably too bourgeois. He always demanded the best. Still does."

"Like this place," I noted, glancing up at the Tiffany-style chandelier over the kitchen island.

By this time, the Italian seasonings in the lasagne were filling the air with a delicious aroma. Holly grabbed a couple of oven mitts and removed the pan from the oven.

While she spooned up two servings, I carried the salad bowl and wine to the table in the dining room.

Pausing a moment, I looked around at the shiny mahogany table, the antique sideboard, and the expensive looking draperies. It was a room fit for royals.

"I can't imagine growing up here." I pulled out a chair at the table which sat twenty guests.

Holly paused in the doorway with a plate in each hand. "We could eat in the kitchen if you'd prefer. It's more casual."

"This is fine," I replied, stretching my leg out. "Just don't sit at the opposite end or we'll have to shout."

Together, we occupied the nearest corner of the table and continued to talk about our childhoods and academic and professional careers.

"You know," she said as she picked up her wine glass and took a sip, "there was a time I wanted to be a cop."

"Really?" That surprised me.

"After something that happened when I was young, I started taking karate lessons to learn how to defend myself. Then I became obsessed with all those police dramas on television. That was a major bone of contention in the house because I was only allowed to watch TV for two hours a week. Weekends only."

I nearly spit out my wine. "Two hours a week?"

"Yes. That's why I got such good grades. I was reading science textbooks while all the other kids were watching *SpongeBob*."

I set my glass down. "Do you still take karate?"

"I'm a third degree black belt," she replied, "and I still practice three times a week."

I raised my glass to clink against hers. "I'm impressed."

We regarded each other over the rims of our wine glasses with a curious intensity as we sipped. By now the pain was gone.

"So what happened when you were younger that made you take karate and watch cop shows?" I set my glass down on the table. "Or do you mind if I take a guess?"

"Go ahead," she replied, watching me with mild amusement.

"I think maybe you and your parents were victims of a break-and-enter situation. You were about thirteen or fourteen and had to lock yourself in the bathroom with your mother. But the police came and you were grateful, and that instilled in you a great respect for the brave officers of the law."

A momentary look of discomfort crossed her face. "How did you know that?"

"How do you think?"

"Leah?"

I nodded soberly.

"Wow." Holly set down her fork and sat back as the reality of the situation sank in.

"She also told me it was your brother Riley who broke into the house," I added, "and that he went to jail afterward."

Holly picked up her fork again and moved the food around on her plate. "It wasn't one of my family's finer moments, that's for sure."

The grandfather clock chimed the hour and we waited for it to finish.

When it grew quiet again, I resumed the thread of our conversation. "Leah spent a lot of time talking to me about Riley," I carefully mentioned. "She told me she regretted not trying to help him when she had the chance, and I promised I'd look him up after I got out of the hospital."

Holly inclined her head. "I can't believe she told you all that. None of us have spoken to Riley since he got out of prison, and he hasn't set foot in this house since the night he broke in. He didn't come to Leah's funeral, but I doubt he even knew she was sick. I certainly didn't call him. How could I? I don't even know where he is or if he's dead or alive. I'm not sure what my mom knows, but it doesn't matter because we don't talk about him."

"That didn't bother you?" I asked. "That he didn't come to Leah's funeral?"

She raised an eyebrow in contemplation. "I had other things on my mind—like how I was going to survive without my older sister. My junkie brother was not a top priority."

Looking down at my plate, I nodded with understanding and thought about whether or not I should even tell Holly what Scott had uncovered about her brother's fate after his release from prison. She didn't sound like she wanted to know, which was exactly how Leah had described the situation.

"It wasn't easy for me to hear about Riley," I explained, "because he was my best friend for a good part of my childhood."

"That makes me sad," she thoughtfully replied. "I never really knew the boy you and Leah must have known. By the time I was old enough to have a conversation with him, he wasn't interested. He had an angry chip on his shoulder every time he walked through the door. I was kind of afraid of him and I think my parents were relieved when he moved out because they didn't want him to be a bad influence on me."

Holly finished her wine, and I reached for the bottle to refill her glass.

"Thank you," she softly replied, though she didn't touch it. She simply sat there, staring at a large framed painting of a sailboat on the wall. I suspected she was thinking of Leah.

I finished my dinner and sat forward with my forearms on the table. "That was delicious. Thank you."

At last, she pulled her gaze from the painting and turned toward me.

"Did you look him up?" she asked. "Did you find out what became of him?"

I thought about the regrets Leah had described. Since that's what brought me here in the first place, I decided to hold nothing back. "Yes, and that's partially the reason why I knocked on your door earlier today, but I expected to relay the information to your sister. She's the one who asked for it."

Holly raised her chin. "Well then. Since it was Leah who sent you on that errand and she's not here to follow up on it, I'll do so in her place."

Recognizing Holly's clear grief over the loss of her sister, I reached into my pocket and withdrew a sheet of paper, which I unfolded, laid down on the table and slid toward her.

"What is this?" Holly asked, picking it up.

"His address and phone number," I replied. "I'll leave it up to you to decide what to do with it, but I can at least tell you what I learned—and most of it was easily accessible information."

She seemed to brace herself emotionally for whatever I was about to reveal.

"After Riley was released from prison and drove out to LA," I said, "he was arrested again for possession and served more time behind bars."

Holly closed her eyes and pinched the bridge of her nose.

"But when he got out," I continued, "he must have decided to clean up his act. As of two months ago, he was living in Montana and working for a construction company. He runs a couple of support groups out of his church—for addicts and family members of addicts. He's married and has two young children, a boy and girl, ages four and two. He and his wife own their own home. His wife is a clerk for an insurance agency."

Holly stared at me with wide eyes, blinked a few times, then abruptly stood up and walked out of the room.

I rose from my chair and followed her to the kitchen. There, I found her leaning against the center island with one hand over her face.

"Are you all right?" I asked, moving closer to lay a hand on her shoulder.

Holly turned and surprised me by wrapping her arms around my neck, burying her face in my shoulder. "I'm so happy to hear this," she sputtered. "Really, I am. But at the same time it's excruciating. It's like a knife in my heart."

"Why?"

"Because he hasn't wanted to call us or see us or introduce his children to us. Or his wife. He must think we're horrible people."

I stood for a moment, running my hand up and down her back, smelling the clean fragrance of her long, silky hair.

Suddenly, the moment Leah placed her newborn baby sister into my arms on Christmas Day came flashing into my heart and mind. It seemed like only yesterday because I'd just relived it in the hospital, yet here she was—a grown woman. Brilliant, beautiful. In my arms again.

Something burst open inside of me and all I wanted to do was protect her. I wanted to spare her from all the pain and unpleasantness of the world. Take care of her forever.

This child I'd held.

A lifetime ago.

No longer a child.

It took me a moment to catch my breath and remind myself that all of those thoughts were ridiculous. Holly certainly didn't need taking care of. She was a Harvard grad and had a third degree black belt in karate. She could kick my ass if she wanted to.

"He would have wanted to move forward, not backward," I offered. "That's why he hasn't tried to contact you. It's not uncommon for addicts to avoid situations that they associate with their lowest moments."

Holly stepped back, sniffed and rubbed her nose with the back of her hand.

"Rationally, I know that," she said. "But it's not easy to be objective when it's your long-lost brother who had his head bashed in by your father when you were thirteen. And when your recently deceased sister comes back from the dead to make sure you have your brother's address and phone number. If that's what actually happened. I still don't understand any of this."

She became emotional again and turned into my arms a second time.

I didn't know what to say. All I could do was hold her.

"Will you tell them?" I asked. "Will your parents want to know?"

She stepped back. "I'm not sure. Couldn't they have found out this information on their own if they wanted to? But they didn't. Maybe they assumed the worst—that he was in jail again or dead from an overdose. I'm pretty sure my mother would faint if I told her she had grandchildren she didn't know about. As far as my father is concerned...I honestly don't know how he would react. He might fly into a rage and warn us never to contact Riley or there will be hell to pay."

"What do *you* want to do?" I asked.

Furiously, she wiped away a tear. "I want to see him again. I want to meet my niece and nephew."

"Then that's what you should do," I replied, feeling no regret whatsoever about encouraging her to defy her father's wishes.

I suspected I might come to regret that eventually, but in that moment, Holly was all that mattered.

I wondered what Leah would have thought about all of this, and suspected that maybe she was the one orchestrating it all.

CHAPTER

Thirty-one

❦

I ended up spending the night on Holly's sofa in the front parlor. The following morning she claimed she'd offered me a bed in one of the guest rooms, but apparently, I wouldn't budge when she shook me.

"How late were we up?" I asked as I sat down on one of the kitchen stools while she poured me a cup of coffee.

"I'm not sure," she replied. "The last time I remember the clock chiming, it was 3:00 a.m., but we were still talking at that point. When I went upstairs it was 4:30. I must have dozed off for a while because you were sound asleep beside me."

I remembered the moments leading up to that. She had fallen asleep at the opposite end of the sofa, curled up in a ball with her cheek resting on her hands, and I hadn't wanted to wake her. That's when I must have nodded off, too.

Just then, the grandfather clock in the dining room chimed for 9:00 a.m. and I jumped. "How do you live with that thing?" I asked. "Doesn't it drive you insane?"

"It's been doing that since I was a baby," she explained, taking a seat on the stool beside me. "I don't even hear it."

"You're lucky," I replied, sipping my coffee and thinking about our conversations the night before. We'd talked about everything from favorite music to most embarrassing moments.

There was no question I was fascinated with Holly by then. She seemed to be everywhere in my mind, all at once. It was as if I'd known her forever, which in a way, I suppose I had.

"How do you feel about everything this morning?" I asked, referring to the question of whether or not she would contact Riley, or tell her parents about it.

"I'm still not sure," she replied. "I know I want to see him, but I don't know how Dad will react to that. I'm pretty sure Mom will fall to pieces and want to see her grandchildren, but will she be able to stand up to my dad if he says no? Will she do it anyway?"

The telephone rang. Holly stood to answer it.

"Hello? Oh hi," she said in a familiar half whisper, turning her back to me. "Did you get home okay? How was the flight? Any delays?"

I waited patiently while she carried on a quiet conversation about airports, work, and how she was coping.

Slowly, as she continued to talk in quiet tones, a tight knot took form in my stomach. I couldn't help but draw some conclusions about the person on the other end of the line. I raised my coffee cup to my lips and downed what was left of it, then set it on the counter and slid it away from me.

At last she hung up the phone. I swallowed heavily over my rising disappointment.

"Sorry about that," she said, blushing slightly as she returned to the stool beside me. She picked up her mug and took a sip, then glanced around the kitchen, unable to meet my gaze.

"Boyfriend?" I asked, raising my eyebrows.

"Yes." She shrugged her shoulder, somewhat apologetically. "He was here for Leah's funeral and just flew home yesterday."

"Where's home?"

I wondered how long he'd been gone before I'd knocked on her door. *Hours? Minutes?*

Just thinking about that made me want to knock my head against a wall a few times. What was it about me and women I was attracted to? There always seemed to be some other guy...

Holly nervously cleared her throat. "Dallas. He's doing a residency there."

Another doctor? Great.

Since I had no claim on this woman, all I could do was make light of it. I leaned forward and grinned. "What is it about this family? Don't you people know how to mix and mingle with the rest of the world? With those of us without medical credentials?"

To my relief, she laughed and covered her mouth with a fist, as if she was afraid of spraying coffee all over me. "Maybe it's because I didn't watch enough *SpongeBob* episodes as a kid. Clearly my world is far too small."

"Maybe you need to live in a pineapple under the sea for a while."

Holly laughed again and the clock pendulum clicked steadily in the other room. The humor of the moment faded quickly, however. The mood turned melancholy. Again, I knew she was thinking of Leah.

"What's his name?" I gently asked.

"Paul."

"How did you meet him?"

"Med school," she told me. "He was in his final year, I was just starting. Thanks to my dad—who made a few calls on Paul's behalf—he got into a great neurosurgery program in Dallas, which is exactly what Paul always wanted. He's from Texas originally."

"I see." I nodded my head in an exaggerated manner. "Your dad must *love* him. He probably has a church and reception hall already picked out for the perfect date in June."

Holly gave me a warning look. "I would tell you to behave yourself, but you're probably right. Dad adores him. He thinks he's the cat's meow."

I detected a hint of cynicism in her tone as I watched her sip her coffee.

"What do *you* think?" I asked. "Will there be a June wedding?"

Holly sighed. "Not after everything that happened with Leah. I don't think it would be wise for me to make any major life decisions right now." She continued to hug her coffee mug in both hands. "Now that I think about it, it's been that way for the past couple of years, ever since Leah was diagnosed. All I could do was keep gliding along. I feel like I've been living my life on auto-pilot."

I stood up to refill my coffee cup, at least relieved to hear that Holly wasn't tempted to rush into anything. "So is it serious with this guy?"

"I suppose."

Returning to my stool and wondering why she hadn't mentioned a significant other the night before when we were up all night talking, I set my mug on the counter. "That kind of sounds like an auto-pilot response."

We gazed at each other intently, then she let out a sigh. "He's an amazing man, Josh. Really. Smart, handsome, responsible. I'm very lucky."

"But…" I prodded, leaning forward and feeling not the least bit guilty about urging her to rethink things.

What the hell was I doing? I'd just come out of a relationship with a woman who wanted to be with another man whose neck

I wanted to wring. Now I was trying to become that "other guy" who couldn't keep his hands off a woman who was already taken?

Holly set down her cup.

"What's his family like?" I asked.

"His father owns an investment firm so they're very well off. His mother didn't have a career, though she sometimes does volunteer work. They're a lot like my own parents I suppose."

I nodded in understanding, and we quietly finished our coffees.

"I should probably get going," I said, though I didn't really want to leave, but it seemed the appropriate thing to say in that moment. "Thanks for the dinner and the use of your sofa. I enjoyed talking to you." I rose to my feet.

"I enjoyed talking to you, too." Holly followed me to the back hall where my jacket hung on a hook. "But some of the things we talked about still seem so…unanswered."

"You mean about Riley?" I asked as I slid my arms into the sleeves of my jacket.

"And Leah," she replied. "What happened to you during your surgery was incredible all on its own, but then you talked to my sister—if that's what really happened. I don't know how you're getting by without knowing what it all means. Whether it was real or not. Part of me thinks we should put you in a lab and do experiments on you."

"That sounds like a whole lot of fun." We walked to the front door. "You know, it's strange," I said, pausing on the braided rug. "A month ago, I never gave a single thought to heaven or the idea that we might actually have souls. I'll admit I was arrogant about that kind of thing. I thought people who believed in their "higher selves" weren't operating on all four cylinders. I thought I knew everything about who and what we are—that when we die,

it's game over; pure nothingness—but now I feel completely...
humbled. At the same time, I think I saw things most people can't
even dream of. Maybe that's arrogant too."

Holly gazed at me, looking bewildered.

"I should get going," I said again when she made no comment.

Moving to the door, I waited for her to open it, then stepped
out onto the covered porch.

"Will you let me know if you're going to get in touch with
Riley? I'd like to see him myself, but I don't want to get in your
way."

Holly stood in the doorway, holding the screen door open.
"I'll keep you posted. The first thing I need to do is talk to my
parents and tell them what you told me. See how they feel about
moving forward. And you have my cell number, right?"

I nodded. "And you have mine? Call or text any time, Holly,
because Lord knows I've got nothing else to do for the next five
weeks."

She smiled and waved good-bye as I walked down the steps,
going easy on my sore leg, as best I could.

C H A P T E R

Thirty-two

That night, I dreamed I was back at work, alone in a squad car, pursuing a speeding black vehicle on the Interstate.

Rain came down in buckets and I could barely see through the water sloshing down my windshield.

I increased the wiper speed and they beat back and forth in front of me like two upside-down clock pendulums, but nothing could clear away the watery blur.

I was driving dangerously fast. Though I gripped the steering wheel tightly in both hands until my knuckles turned white, I still felt as if I had no control. I feared that at any second, my tires would skid and I would spin around a dozen times and tumble down the embankment.

Suddenly the guy I was chasing hit the brakes. His vehicle flipped over and flew into the air. Everything seemed to happen in slow motion as I drove under his airborne car and looked up at the under-carriage—like an airplane over my head.

It was a mistake to take my attention off the road, because the instant I faced forward again, I slammed my foot on the brake pedal to avoid a woman pushing a baby carriage across the street.

It was too late. My front grill collided with the carriage. It flew up into the air, over my head—just like the speeding vehicle.

The baby, swaddled in a white blanket, landed on the hood of my car and bounced across the windshield.

I woke in a panic, sat bolt upright. *"No!"*

Breathing heavily, I lay a hand on my bare chest. My heart was pounding like a drum. I was completely drenched in sweat.

Taking a few deep, slow breaths, I lay back down and blinked up at the ceiling. Why did I dream that? What did it mean?

After a few minutes, I knew I couldn't go back to sleep, so I switched on the light and got up.

Release

Thirty-three

Holly James

It's funny how some days are dull and unremarkable—a small fleck of gray in the tapestry of your life—while others are like explosions of color that can define your entire existence, from the moment of your birth until you draw your last breath.

The day Josh Wallace walked through my door and spent the night on my sofa turned out to be one of those days.

Or maybe the word "explosion" is putting it too mildly.

Thirty-four

Since I'd already taken three weeks off from school to remain at Leah's bedside during her final days, attend her funeral and hobble through the initial stages of my grief, I knew I couldn't continue to avoid school much longer. After Josh left that Sunday morning, I sent an email to one of my instructors and asked what would be happening on Monday.

I was told there would be a brief oral exam on obstetrics. He gave me the option to postpone, but since I had the entire day to prepare and I was a rock star when it came to hitting the books, I promised to be there.

Three hours later, I sat at the desk in my room eating a bowl of leftover lasagne when a car door slammed shut outside. Rising from my chair, I crossed to the window, pushed the lace curtain aside with my finger, and looked down at the driveway below.

My parents were unpacking the car and heading for the door with their suitcases.

"Darn it," I whispered, glancing back at my dirty bowl of lasagne on the desk and wondering where I was going to hide it, because there were very strict rules in the house about taking food up to the bedrooms.

All my life I'd followed those rules without challenging them—I'd seen what happened to Riley; it really wasn't worth the fight—but if there was an opportunity to do what I wanted when my parents were away, I seized it. Afterward, I cleaned up my mess so no one was the wiser...But suddenly here they were, home earlier than expected, and my room smelled like an Italian restaurant.

I thought about shoving the dirty bowl under my bed, lowering the dust ruffle and opening the window to let some fresh air blow through—but something in me felt different that day. At the time, I thought maybe it was my stress levels due to the exam. Or maybe something inside me had changed after losing my sister. Suddenly, stupid details like where food could be consumed within the house seemed rather irrelevant in the grand scheme of things.

Or maybe I was just cranky and defiant from drinking too much coffee.

In the end, it didn't matter. Knowing I should go downstairs to welcome my parents home, I decided to proudly carry my lasagne bowl to the kitchen without trying to sneak it past my father's notice.

That decision turned out to be a grave mistake.

Or maybe it was the smartest thing I'd ever done.

"Welcome home," I cheerfully said as I descended the red carpeted stairs with dirty dishes in my hands.

My father stopped in the main hall and set down his suitcase. "What is that?" he asked.

As if befuddled by the question, I regarded my cup and bowl and held them out for him to see. "You mean *these*?"

His expression became a mask of stone. "Yes, *those*. Did you take food up to your room?"

I pursed my lips. "Yes, I did. I was studying for an exam and I was hungry."

He took a few steps forward and spoke in a tone that conveyed his shock and disappointment in me. "You know the rules, Holly. Why would you do that?"

"Because I was hungry," I explained a second time, moving past him to the kitchen. I pulled open the dishwasher door and placed the items inside.

"But there are *rules*," he reminded me yet again, for the millionth time in my life. "Even when your mother and I are not at home, they still apply, and there are reasons for those rules."

"Like what?" I demanded.

"Like getting stains on furniture, or attracting mice or insects. But that's not really the point, Holly. Without rules that everyone agrees to respect, things can degenerate into pure chaos."

I gestured toward the dishwasher. "I'm not a total slob, Dad. I had a napkin on my lap and we do have laundry facilities if, heaven forbid, a drop of tomato sauce should land on a bedspread."

With that, I moved to the kitchen doorway to hug my mother. "Hi Mom. I'm glad you're home. Did you have a nice time?"

"Oh well, you know…" She was, of course, alluding to the fact that we were all still grieving deeply over Leah. "It was nice to just be quiet for a few days, come to terms with everything—though I don't know if I'll ever truly be able to do that."

I drew back to look at her in the late afternoon light. "It's going to take time for all of us. We just have to be here for each other."

She pulled me into her arms again and I was vaguely aware of my father moving past us to carry the suitcases upstairs.

A short while later, we stood around the kitchen island while Mom made turkey sandwiches for herself and Dad.

"Did Paul make it home all right?" my father asked, surprising me by letting the food-in-the-bedroom issue go without doling out consequences.

"Yes," I replied. "He called this morning. Smooth flight. No delays."

"Glad to hear it. And what's the exam on tomorrow?"

"Obstetrics."

"Are you ready for it?"

"Not yet," I admitted, "but I still have the rest of the day to prepare."

Mom sliced both sandwiches diagonally. "Don't you have a karate class later?" she asked.

Using a fork to draw a pickle out of the jar, I took it between my fingers and crunched into it. "I do, but I'll need a break by then."

"Are you sure?" Dad asked. "You're taking a break now. Maybe you should skip the class."

I shook my head. "No. I'm going."

He regarded me with puzzled displeasure.

We all sat down on the stools around the large center island while Mom and Dad ate their sandwiches and told me about their weekend on the Cape. I waited until the right moment, then carefully broached the subject that was foremost on my mind.

"There's something I need to talk to you about." I rested my chin on my hand. "Something happened yesterday while you were gone. We had an unexpected guest."

"Really? Who?" Mom asked.

"An old friend of Riley's," I explained. "Do you remember Josh Wallace? They were best friends when they were kids. He was the cop who was shot during that carjacking that happened when Leah was…" I couldn't bring myself to finish the sentence. "You mentioned that you knew him when you saw the news."

"Josh from Sycamore Street," Mom said. "Yes, of course. I felt terrible about that, but we were so preoccupied. Is he all right now? Did he come to pay his respects?"

I wasn't comfortable talking about Josh's near-death experience without his permission, so I decided not to mention that he hadn't even known Leah had passed.

"That's right," I replied. "He came to the door after Paul left and I invited him in."

"You invited him in?" My father seemed concerned.

I swiveled on the stool to meet his gaze. "Why wouldn't I?"

"Because he's a total stranger and you were home alone."

I couldn't help but chuckle somewhat cynically. "First of all, I'm not twelve. I can handle a guest at the door. Second, he's not a stranger, Dad. He was your neighbor once."

My father pointed a finger at me. "And that boy was trouble. Don't get me started about the times I came home late at night to find the cops parked out front because of that kid's antics. He was a terrible influence on Riley."

"I don't think you can blame what happened to Riley on a friend he had when he was ten," I argued. "Correct me if I'm wrong, but wasn't it the other group of friends he made when he moved *here* that caused all the trouble?"

Dad picked up the other half of his sandwich and took a bite out of it. "I suppose they all had a hand in it, in different ways."

For a moment I watched him chew, then something in me snapped. I couldn't explain it. It never happened before, but I simply couldn't control what came out of my mouth next.

"As if you had no hand in it at all?" I boldly asked.

My father swallowed. "Excuse me?"

"You heard what I said. I just think we all have to take responsibility for what happened to Riley, because this house wasn't the easiest place to grow up in, especially as a teenager."

Slowly setting down his sandwich, my father slid the plate away, leaned forward in an intimidating manner, rested his elbows on the island countertop and folded his hands together.

"I do take responsibility for what happened to my son. Lord knows there are things I could have done differently and I'll have to live with that, but I don't appreciate your tone, Holly. Nor do I want to talk about your brother after what we've just been through with your sister."

"But isn't that why we *should* talk about it?" I asked. "We just lost Leah and suddenly I feel like an only child, but I'm not. I have a brother out there somewhere and you have a son. Yet we're not allowed to talk about him."

"For good reason," Dad said. "He's a criminal. And this subject is too hard on your mother. She's lost two children. Have a little compassion, will you?"

I breathed deeply. "What if Riley wasn't a criminal? What if I had information about him?" I turned to face my mother who had remained silent thus far. "That's what I want to tell you about. When Josh came by, he asked about Riley. He knew he spent time in jail, and then he told me that he had looked him up."

My mother's eyes grew wide. "And…?"

I took both her hands in mine. "It's good news. It sounds like Riley has turned his life around. I'm not sure if you knew that he spent more time in jail when he got to LA, but now he's living in Montana, holding down a steady job, and he's married."

My mother blinked a few times. "Married. Since when?"

"I'm not sure exactly, but he and his wife have two young children—a boy and a girl, ages four and two."

My mother's eyes immediately filled with tears. Covering her mouth with a hand, she turned to my father.

There was no doubt in my mind that these were tears of joy, but my father didn't appear too happy to hear any of this. He smacked the countertop with his open palm, which caused me to jump.

"Do you see what you're doing?" He rose to his feet. "We don't need this right now, Holly."

"Why *not* now?" I retorted. "This is *good* news, Dad. You have two grandchildren and I have a niece and a nephew. And Riley's okay."

"We don't know that," he argued. "We don't know *anything* about the situation. First of all, let me point out that he's never been able to stay clean for long, and have you forgotten the filth and disgrace he brought on this family? The danger he put us all in? I swear to God, as long as I live and breathe, that boy will never set foot in this house again, and you will not make contact with him. I don't want him back in our lives. Do you understand?"

"You can't tell me what to do," I argued, also rising to my feet. "I'm a grown woman and I don't care what Riley did in the past. He's my brother and I want to see him—that is...if he'll even allow me to see him. I honestly have no idea because he's never tried to contact us, and that breaks my heart."

My mother was now quietly weeping. I wasn't sure if she was crying because of the heated argument in her kitchen, or if she was still shedding tears of joy over learning that Riley was okay.

"Mom," I gently said, laying a hand on her shoulder. "I'm sorry. I didn't mean to upset you."

"You didn't," she replied. "I'm just so happy to hear he's all right and that he's found someone. A *wife*. All these years, I thought maybe he was dead."

"He's not dead. He's very much alive and I'm going to write to him."

"No, you will *not*," my father stipulated. "I told you, I don't want him back in our lives."

"Well, it's not up to you, is it?" I insisted. "The last time I checked, it was a free country and I want to see my brother."

A muscle twitched at his jaw. "Not while you're living under my roof, you won't."

I scoffed in disbelief. "So let me get this straight. Are you telling me I *can't*, and that if I disobey you, you'll cut me off? Kick me out?"

It wasn't something I was keen to risk because med school didn't come cheap. Without the financial support of my family—not to mention the free rent I enjoyed while living at home—I could never have made it this far. I did not fail to appreciate those facts.

Which is why I never rocked the boat when it came to my father's ridiculous house rules. Until now.

Without waiting for him to reply, I walked out of the kitchen and strode upstairs to my room. Quietly closing the door behind me, I looked around at the space I'd occupied all my life, except for the few years I'd spent in residence during undergrad before Leah got sick. That's why I'd decided to move home, to help care for her and spend as much time as possible with her before the end came.

Now she was gone and the house felt agonizingly empty.

I stood there, heart racing, blood rushing through my veins, and fought the urge to pick up my laptop and throw it against the wall, then rip my curtains off the rods and do all of that while screaming my head off in a wild, hysterical rage.

Instead, I grabbed my karate gear out of the closet, stuffed my textbooks and laptop into the gym bag, and hurried downstairs.

My parents said nothing as I stormed past the kitchen. I think they were in shock because I'd never talked back to my father before.

Twenty minutes later, I was sitting in my car outside the dojo, waiting impatiently for class to begin because I needed a good workout. I needed to focus my thoughts on something other than my anger toward my father.

It was strange and rather telling that I didn't call Paul to tell him about my argument with Dad. Instead, I dug out my phone and texted Josh.

CHAPTER

Thirty-six

It's funny. Sometimes when you're passionate about something and you dedicate yourself to it completely, your actions become a reflex. Your senses become more astute and time slows down before your eyes.

A seasoned basketball player might see a hoop that looks gigantic to him and all his shots swish through the net. In karate, there are moments when everything happens in slow motion and it's as if you have an eternity to react.

If only life could be like that.

A few minutes before the end of class, Jim came at me with a massive loud, "*Kia!*" He lunged aggressively with a punch to my face—as he'd done a thousand times before.

With a flick of my wrist, his strike and all his momentum was thrown off. I grabbed his shoulder, kicked his leg out from under him and dropped him flat on his face.

Before he had a chance to register what had occurred, I punched at the back of his head with a forceful yell, stopping within an inch. In karate, it's called 'going in for the kill.'

Though we were both breathing hard, Jim rolled over onto his back with a big smile. "Nice."

I wiped the perspiration from my brow, grinned down at him and offered my hand to help him up.

In that instant, something caught my eye near the door. It was Josh, dressed in a black leather jacket, his hands buried deep in the pockets of his faded blue jeans. He was leaning casually against the door jamb, watching me.

Tall, dark, broad-shouldered and fit, he was hands down, by far, the most attractive man I'd ever laid eyes on. I'd thought so the moment I opened my door to find him standing on my front porch the previous day, but I'd been suffering a very low moment of grief and wasn't inclined to swoon at any man's feet.

When I'd covered him with the blanket on my parents' sofa at 4:30 that morning, I must have stared at him, enraptured, for a full ten minutes before finally going off to bed.

Now here he was again, waiting to talk to me, and I could barely catch my breath—which had nothing to do with my workout. Our eyes met, and it happened again. Time seemed to stand still, my blood slowed to a smooth pulsing motion in my veins and I felt a strange, relaxing warmth flow to all my extremities.

"You know that guy?" Jim asked as I realized he was staring at Josh, too.

"Yeah, he's an old family friend." Though one could argue I'd only just met him the day before.

"Too bad you didn't notice him standing there sixty seconds ago or you would have been the one landing on your face just now."

I smiled and nudged Jim in the ribs with my forearm. "Go take a shower."

"No, *you* take a shower," he replied, "and better make it a cold one."

"You're bad," I teased as he sauntered off to the locker room.

In bare feet, dressed in my white, black-belted Gi, I took a deep breath and stepped off the blue practice mat. Strolling slowly to meet Josh at the edge of the floor, I struggled to find the right, socially appropriate words to greet him.

"Thanks for coming," I said.

"Thanks for texting me," he replied, then he gestured toward the blue mats. "That was impressive. Would it be wrong of me to say I'm incredibly turned on right now?"

The mere sound of his voice caused my blood to quicken. "Would it be wrong to say I'm incredibly flattered?"

"No," he replied with some amusement. "Want to get out of here?"

"Definitely. If you don't mind waiting for me to take a quick shower?"

His chest rose and fell with a heavy, teasing sigh. "I'll do my best to be patient."

And I'll do my best to keep my head on straight, I thought as I made my way to the locker room.

"**D**id he really say that?" Josh asked as we slid into a booth at a nearby diner. "That you weren't *permitted* to contact Riley?"

"That's right," I replied. "You'd think, after losing Leah, he might want to reconcile with the son he also lost. Like a second chance. It boggles my mind that he doesn't see it that way."

"From what I recall," Josh said, "he was always pretty hard on Riley."

The waitress arrived, placed two plastic-covered menus in front of us and poured us some water. She took our drink orders and left us alone for a few minutes.

"What are you going to do?" Josh asked. "Will you still try and get in touch with him?"

"Of course," I replied, "and I told my father that. I think he was shocked because it was the first time I ever talked back to him. Then he threatened me with the old cliché: 'Not while you're living under *my* roof.' I'm not sure how serious he was about that."

I continued to read over the menu.

"Are you worried?" Josh asked.

"Strangely, no," I replied. "Though I probably should be because he's been paying my tuition and letting me live at home rent free for the past couple of years." I read over the soup and salad choices. "At the same time, I'm twenty-five years old. Maybe I should just move out and get my own bank loan. Then at least I wouldn't feel like I was wearing a yoke around my neck."

"It's always an option," Josh agreed. "I'm sure a bank would give you a loan, considering your future career prospects."

With a resigned sigh, I set the menu down on the table. "I really don't want to go home and face more arguments, so thanks for having dinner with me."

"No problem," he replied. "I just want to make sure you're okay."

"Believe me, I am. Actually, I feel an incredible sense of release—like I was a pressure cooker for the past ten years and someone just lifted the lid."

"I hope it wasn't me," he casually mentioned, "because your father always considered me a delinquent. He probably thinks it was me who encouraged you to rebel."

"It doesn't matter. But that's exactly what it was, you know," I replied indulgently. *"A beautiful rebellion.* I had this overwhelming, burning urge to defy him. I couldn't stop myself. After years of biting my tongue, I had to let it all out. Now I understand how Riley must have felt and why he constantly rebelled."

"While you girls always toed the line."

"Mmm." I sipped my water and thought about that. "I hate to think we were just submissive. I don't think that's what it was."

"What do you think it was, then?"

I shrugged. "Maybe we instinctively knew it was wiser to follow the rules in order to keep the peace, while Riley was the type who liked to poke at a hornet's nest just to see what would happen." I reached for my water and sipped it. "When it comes to personality types, my father is definitely a hornet's nest."

"How so?"

"Probably because of how he was raised. It might surprise you to know that he came from very humble beginnings. I saw a picture of his house once. It was nothing but a shack somewhere out in the boonies of Kentucky. He had eight brothers and sisters and his father was a drunk who beat everyone to within an inch of their lives if they misbehaved, or for no reason at all, I was told. He would come home from the bar, look around at everyone, and just lose it. Mom said that Dad was quite a scrapper with his brothers when he was younger, but when he told her about all that, he promised never to be an abusive husband. I guess he felt that promise didn't apply to his son."

"I didn't know about that," Josh said. "Have you ever met your father's parents?"

"No, and they're both long gone now. He doesn't even keep in touch with his brothers or sisters. I think they're all still back there. He was the only one who got out and forged a different kind of life. He keeps it pretty quiet, though. Considers it a major skeleton in our closet. That and Riley. When he meets people, he just says he has two daughters."

The waitress returned with our sodas and took our food orders. We each chose the same thing: a burger and fries, extra ketchup, no onions.

After the waitress left, we leaned forward over the table. "It's weird," I said. "Even though you and I barely know each other, I feel like you understand the situation better than anyone."

"I don't know about that," Josh replied, unpretentiously. "But I'm glad you texted me because you were the only thing I could think about today. You and this very strange situation."

I was half tempted to reach across the table and touch his hand—he had such strong, manly hands—but I resisted.

"It is strange," I agreed. "I had a hard time concentrating, too. I'm worried about that exam tomorrow."

"Sorry. Guess I am a bad influence after all."

"No." I shook my head.

"Is there any way I can help?" he asked. "You could study at my place if you don't want to go home. I could quiz you or something. At the very least I could bring you coffee."

"That would be helpful, actually," I replied.

"Which part? The quizzing or the coffee?"

"Both. It's an oral exam where we're put in a situation with a fake patient who presents symptoms and we have to diagnose. You could be the patient. And bring me coffee, too."

He inclined his head curiously. "Are you saying we'll be playing doctor this evening?"

"That's exactly what we'll be doing." I couldn't help but laugh.

Josh sat back and held his hands up in surrender. "Then I'm definitely your guy."

Unfortunately for Josh, playing doctor didn't turn out quite like he'd expected because I asked him to mimic symptoms of an ectopic pregnancy and various other female ailments, as it was an obstetrics and gynecology exam. He was a good sport nonetheless, and quizzed me on a number of facts and unique case studies from my notes.

My mother texted me around 11:00 to ask if I was okay. I assured her I was fine and staying with a friend.

She didn't ask the name of the friend and I wondered if she suspected it was Josh. If so, I hoped she wouldn't mention that to my father or he might storm over here with a SWAT team to rescue me from what he would surely perceive as a hostage situation.

Josh and I studied until 3:00 a.m., then he insisted that I take his bed while he slept on the sofa. He rose early the next morning to make me a veggie and cheese omelette with coffee, and sent me out the door with a packed lunch to get me through the day.

❧

Despite all my valiant efforts, the exam that morning was a train wreck. I'd never performed so badly at anything in my life.

Afterward I had to apologize to my instructor for my embarrassing lack of knowledge and uncharacteristic hesitations.

It wasn't that I hadn't worked hard to prepare, I tried to explain, but clearly I'd missed a lot of material over the past few weeks. And yes, I was distracted because of my grief over losing my sister and the argument I'd just had with my parents. I told him about that too.

Josh had been a distraction as well, but I left that part out. I didn't admit that no matter how hard I tried, I couldn't stop thinking about him. He was in and out of my head every minute of the day, both during and after the exam. I replayed the details of all our conversations and thought about things I didn't know about him yet and wanted to ask. I also envisioned the night he was shot after stopping the carjacker on the side of the road.

I thought of him dying on the operating table.

Had he really seen and spoken to Leah? Or was he suffering from PTSD, and was I equally unstable to go along with him for the ride?

These thoughts and questions consumed me, but I couldn't afford to take any more time off from school. I had no choice but to force myself to purge all those thoughts from my mind as best I could and stay focused on medicine.

It was just past 6:00 p.m. when I got into my car, closed my eyes, and rested my forehead on the steering wheel.

"You need to go home," I whispered to myself. "Go home and be normal again."

If only it could have been so easy, but the "normal life" I once knew didn't seem to exist anymore. For one thing, Leah was gone. On top of that, I couldn't go on pretending to be content with an existence in my father's house where I was expected to follow his rules and not think or choose anything for myself.

Over the past forty-eight hours, I'd learned things I couldn't erase from my mind—like the fact that Leah might have come back from the dead to use Josh as a messenger to deliver information about Riley.

Or the fact that there might truly be an afterlife. Would this count as legitimate proof?

Suddenly my phone vibrated in my purse and I jumped. Lifting my head from the steering wheel, I pulled the phone out, swiped a finger across the screen and read the message. It was from Paul: *Hey there. Want to Skype tonight?*

Normally I would have said sure, what time? But something resembling a severe claustrophobic response came over me, and I didn't even want to deal with figuring out how to reply. So I stuffed the phone back into my purse and started the engine.

This much I knew: I didn't want to go home.

All I wanted to do was see Josh.

I wasn't surprised when it took Josh awhile to answer the doorbell. He probably had a hard time getting up from chairs and the stairway was a long one.

At least he was home. I knew that because I could see the lights on in the upstairs windows.

"Sorry I didn't call first," I said when he finally opened the door and found me standing on the step. "I hope it's okay...just showing up like this. You're probably worried I'm going to turn into some freeloader or something but I promise I won't. I just couldn't go home again. I couldn't deal with my father today."

Josh took hold of my elbow and gently pulled me inside. "Come in. You're shivering."

"Am I?" I hadn't even realized.

"Where's you're coat?" He looked out the door for my car, which I'd parked down the street. "And the rest of your stuff?"

It wasn't until that moment that I glanced down at myself. It was a chilly evening. A cold damp fog had rolled into the harbor and I only wore jeans and a tank top.

"I must have left my purse in the front seat," I absent-mindedly replied. "Gosh, I don't even remember driving over here. I'm a mess."

He rubbed at the tops of my arms and shoulders to warm them. "Go upstairs and get a sweatshirt out of one of my drawers. I'll get your stuff. Do you have your car keys?"

I opened my palm and held them out. "At least I didn't leave them in the ignition. Always a bright side, right?"

He took them from me and waited while I climbed the stairs. "Make yourself comfortable," he said. "I'll be right back."

Five minutes later, I was seated on Josh's leather sofa staring numbly at CNN on the flat screen TV and feeling guilty about not replying to Paul's text. It wasn't like me to avoid talking to him.

The front door opened. I immediately rose.

"I shouldn't have asked you to do that," I said as I met Josh at the top of the stairs. "Your leg…Are you okay?"

"It's good for me," he replied. "I need to exercise it." He handed me my purse and carried my jacket and backpack to the chair in the living room. "So the exam didn't go so well?"

I shook my head. "I missed a lot while I was away. It's okay, though. I'm not going to flunk out or anything. My instructor knows the circumstances. He said there would be plenty of time to make it up."

Josh gestured toward me. "I see you found a sweatshirt?"

"Yes. Thank you."

"Are you hungry?"

"Not really."

He studied my face for a moment. "You look like you need to eat, Holly. I could make you a grilled cheese sandwich."

I lay a hand on my belly and realized it was growling like a beast. "That sounds good, actually."

As I followed Josh into the kitchen, all thoughts about that unanswered text from Paul floated out of my mind. All I wanted to do was relax and think of other things for a while.

Forty

J osh made two sandwiches—one for each of us. He also set a bottle of honey mustard on the table for dipping, which turned out to be a delicious surprise.

"Thank you," I said with a sigh as we finished. "That really hit the spot."

"*Poof.*" He waved a hand. "All the troubles of the day disappear."

"I wish," I replied.

With a nod of understanding, he carried the plates to the sink. "Let's go sit down for a bit."

Anticipation rose in my chest—a strange, joyful energy that had been a distraction all day long. It was why I felt compelled to come here tonight.

Sliding my chair back, I followed him into the living room where we sat facing each other at opposite ends of the sofa. I folded one leg up under me, rested my cheek on a hand.

"I don't know how I'd be surviving all this without you," I said.

"When in fact," he replied, "none of it would even be happening if not for me. Maybe you should be yelling at me right now."

I softly laughed. "You're right. You're like a grenade someone threw into my world." I pondered that for a moment. "Was it

Leah who pulled the pin and pitched it? Or is it crazy for me to even think that? Now I'm starting to wonder if maybe I'm the one who needs therapy because everyone knows…there's no such thing as ghosts."

Josh nodded. "I know what you're saying. I'm still not sure I didn't dream the whole thing, even though it felt real. I've been trying to tell myself it was a hallucination because of the pain killers and the coma. That's a lot easier to accept. And everything did feel a bit surreal whenever she was in the room. At least it seems that way looking back on it."

"How will we ever know?" I asked him. "It's not like you can prove it was real, to yourself or anyone else. If we're going to play devil's advocate, maybe what you learned about Riley was in your subconscious somehow because you'd seen or heard things that didn't register at the time. But still…I find myself looking around, stopping and listening, wondering if Leah is nearby, watching over me. I feel her sometimes, but maybe I just don't want to let her go. Maybe I'm floating in a sea of grief where I can't see the shore." I stared at the wall for a moment, then completely fell apart and shed some tears.

Josh gathered me into his arms.

"You must think I'm a total basket case," I said, hiccupping as I labored to collect myself.

"You buried your sister a week ago," he gently replied. "Give yourself a break. This is normal, and I'm sorry if I've made things complicated." He continued to rub his hand over my shoulder. "You know what else is strange?"

I wiped a finger under my nose and peered up at him. "What?"

"I'm glad I got shot."

I pulled away and managed a smile as I wiped the tears from eyes. "That *is* strange."

"It hurt like hell, of course," he continued, "but now that I'm sitting here, I think it was worth it."

He pulled me into his arms again and I leaned into the strength of his upper body. His shirt smelled clean, like it had just been laundered. I breathed in the intoxicating scent as if my life depended on it.

As he stroked his hand lightly over my back, I closed my eyes and relaxed while a tremendous sense of well-being washed over me.

How odd…I'd just buried my sister, yet I felt like I was floating.

"How is it possible you're not in a relationship?" I asked Josh a short while later when he returned to the sofa with a roll of tissue from the bathroom—because my eyes were as puffy as cotton balls.

"I guess I've had a run of bad luck," he replied as he handed me the roll and sat down again.

I tore off a long section and blew my nose, then wiped both my eyes. "How so?"

"Dear, sweet Mother of God, where to begin…" He smiled at me. "If you really want to know the embarrassing truth, there's an engagement ring sitting in a box in a drawer in my bedroom because I was fool enough to want to propose to a woman who was in love with another guy."

I set the roll of tissue on the coffee table. "That sucks. When did it happen?"

"She dumped me the same day I got shot," Josh said.

My head drew back in astonishment. "You're kidding."

"No, and maybe that's why I was so reckless that night. I wasn't suicidal or anything, but I was definitely wound up."

"How long were you with her?"

"About a year, but it's a bizarre story."

By this time, we were sitting close, facing each other on the sofa. I lay my hand on Josh's thigh. "Tell me?"

He took a deep breath and let it out. "You sure?" I nodded. "All right. Her name was Carla and she was married before and had a daughter, but her supposed-to-be husband had died in a plane crash somewhere up north in Canada. After we'd been together for a while, she got a call saying that they'd found him alive, floating on an iceberg somewhere in the North Atlantic, so she had to fly up there and be with him in the hospital. But as it turned out, it wasn't her husband after all, but some other passenger on the plane who had her husband's belongings."

"That's horrible," I said.

"Yeah. It was pretty rough on her. Then she fell in love with the guy after only a couple of days and decided she needed to be with him instead of me."

I clasped Josh's hand. "I'm so sorry."

"It's all right," he replied with a shrug. "I took it pretty hard at first, but then I woke up from the coma and something like that puts everything in perspective, you know? You just feel grateful to be alive and you start to understand what's meant to be—or not meant to be."

His expression stilled and grew serious. I wondered if perhaps he wasn't truly over this woman, or at least he hadn't gotten over the betrayal.

"I'm sorry it didn't work out."

He nodded. "What about Paul? I can't imagine he'd be too happy if he could see you right now, sitting with me, especially if he knew you were probably going to spend the night here."

"That's bold," I said, secretly impressed by Josh's confidence.

"I didn't mean it that way," he replied with a slow, boyish grin. "I fully intend to sleep on the sofa again."

I smiled. "I'm not worried about that, but you're right. I should be calling him. He texted me earlier and like a coward, I stuffed the phone back into my purse."

"Why?"

"Because I just didn't feel like replying. Which makes me feel guilty because he's such a good guy. I don't know why I'm avoiding talking to him, but it was a rough day. All I wanted to do was come here. I'm just not ready to face the world."

Josh inclined his head. "I don't want to hold you back from your responsibilities. I mean, I want to help you. I want to see you and everything, but I don't want to cause problems."

I snuggled closer to rest my head on his shoulder. "You're not causing problems."

I yawned and let my eyes fall closed for a minute. Then I woke some time later with the vague sensation that I was being carried off to bed in the arms of a big man who smelled clean, like the outdoors.

Groggily, I opened my eyes just as Josh set me down on the mattress in his room and covered me with a blanket. "You're very strong," I said.

"And you're light as a feather," he replied in a whisper. "What time do you need to get up?"

"I have an 8:30 class. And I want to send an email to Riley tomorrow."

"I'll knock at 7:00," he replied. "Go to sleep. Don't worry about anything."

That was all I remembered before the sun came up and as promised, there was a light knock at the door.

I was just sitting down on Josh's sofa the following evening, preparing to send an email to Riley, when my phone beeped. It was a text from my mother: *Are you okay? I miss you.*

As soon as I read her message, a heaviness centered in my heart because I knew this was not easy on her. She'd already lost two children. Now I was gone, too—by choice—and she didn't know where I was.

I quickly texted her back: *I'm fine, Mom. I'm staying with a friend, going to classes. I just needed a little space. I love you and I'll be home soon, I promise.*

My throat closed up, and I set the phone down on the sofa beside me.

Almost instantly, it beeped again.

Mom wrote: *I'm glad to hear it. Take the time you need. Looking forward to seeing you soon.*

"What's up?" Josh asked as he sat down beside me.

"It's just Mom," I explained. "She misses me and she's worried."

"Of course she is. She's your mom," he said.

I unfolded the piece of paper which contained Riley's contact information and set it down next to my laptop. "I wonder what they'd do if they knew I was staying at your place," I casually mentioned.

"I expect your dad would march over here and insist that you go straight home, young lady."

Just then, there was a loud banging at the door, and our eyes locked on each other's.

—⟞

"What kind of car does your father drive?" Josh asked as he pulled the curtain aside with a finger and peered down at the street below.

"A black Mercedes coupe."

"That's definitely him and he's double parked."

"He does that all the time." I laid my hand on Josh's shoulder as I rose up on my tiptoes to peer out as well.

He turned to me. "What do you want to do?"

"I don't want you to answer it," I quickly replied, feeling rather horrified by the prospect. "Let him bang on the door until he's red in the face. This is none of his business."

"You're his daughter, which makes it very much his business. He must have seen your car on the street."

"I don't care."

He shot me a look. "Are you sure about that?"

I considered it a moment and relented, but only slightly. "If I thought he was here to make amends and apologize for the things he said the other day, I'd go down there and talk to him, but I can tell by the way he's banging on the door that he just wants to drag me home by the ear."

"I don't know, Holly…" Josh replied.

"This is your apartment. There's no law that says you have to answer the door, is there?"

"No, but he's your father."

"I assure you, if we answer the door, we'll get into some kind of scuffle and he'll end up face down on the pavement with his hands behind his back."

"You think so?"

"I know so."

Josh shook his head and made a move to answer the door regardless, but I grabbed hold of his arm. "Please, I don't want to see him tonight. I'm not ready. I promise I'll talk to him eventually, when I get everything sorted out."

Josh stared at me intently for a moment, then thankfully, he conceded.

We both looked out the window again. My father was descending the steps and returning to his car.

"There, see?" I said. "He's leaving. We're off the hook."

"At least for today." Josh turned to face me. "Now what?"

As I gazed into his deep blue eyes, I felt rather buoyant. "I want to email Riley. I just hope he'll be willing to talk to me."

The last time I saw my brother Riley, I was standing at my bedroom window with a hammering heart and salty tears running down my cheeks.

A nasty argument had just taken place in the kitchen downstairs. Both my father and Riley shouted viciously at each other, something smashed against a wall, and Riley ran out the front door. I watched him cross the yard to the street where he jumped into the open back of a half-ton truck with a noisy muffler and white racing stripes painted down the hood.

I remember all too clearly how I cried myself to sleep that night, hugging my stuffed bunny as if my life depended upon it.

It wasn't until much later that Riley and his buddies broke into our home and my mother and I were forced to hide in the bathroom while we waited for the police to arrive.

I never saw Riley that night. I was only told what had occurred—that Dad frightened them away with a baseball bat and they were arrested somewhere in the vicinity where they'd been hiding in a shed.

I wasn't permitted to attend any court proceedings, nor could I visit Riley in prison. All I had to remember him by were newspaper clippings and a few photo albums from his early childhood.

Today, I doubt I would even recognize my brother if I passed him on the street.

So it was with a strange mixture of trepidation and exhilaration that I clicked on the return email that arrived in my inbox later that night.

The subject line said the following: *Hello from your brother in Montana.*

Discord

Forty-three

cc⁓ɔɔ

Nineteen hours later

Riley's email the night before had been brief and to the point.

You asked how I've been doing, but I can't possibly answer that question in an email. We could talk on the phone if you like, or if you're up for it, you could fly out here for a visit. I'd really like to see you.

I decided in that moment that a phone call would definitely not suffice. Josh helped me check flight times and I quickly emailed Riley back to suggest I'd come the next day. I also asked if I could bring Josh with me. Riley said yes and promised to pick us up at the airport.

After the flight the next morning we walked together toward the baggage claim where Riley had agreed to meet us.

"I can't believe we're doing this," I said to Josh as I wheeled my carry-on bag onto the escalator. "And thank you for coming with me, and for using your air miles. I owe you big time."

Josh stepped onto the escalator behind me, massaged the back of my neck and spoke close in my ear. "Don't be silly. Riley was my best friend for the first ten years of my life so this is important to me, too. Besides, how could I pass up an opportunity to spend three whole days with you?"

The note of flirtation in his voice caused a flock of mad butterflies to swarm in my belly as we descended toward the baggage carousels. I began to wonder what the hell I was doing.

Though I had spoken to Paul on the phone that morning and told him I was flying out to meet my brother in Montana, I'd said nothing about bringing along a friend—namely a handsome police officer who on the day I was born was one of the first people in the world to hold me in his arms. Nor did I mention the fact that I'd spent the past few nights at his apartment. He'd slept on the sofa, mind you, but still...

So far, nothing inappropriate had occurred between us, but only a fool could deny the spark of attraction, the temptation, the intimate connection that had arisen out of nowhere in the first five minutes of our acquaintance.

I was attracted to Josh—overwhelmingly so—which was a clear and irrefutable betrayal of Paul's trust. I didn't feel good about it and I certainly wasn't ready to throw away everything I'd built with Paul over the past year. Besides that, Josh was a man who had been ready to propose to another woman a few short weeks ago, a man who had been shot recently in the line of duty, a man who believed he'd gone to heaven and spoken personally with my deceased sister. Was I out of my mind to think any of this was normal?

"I'm not sure I'll even recognize Riley," I said to Josh as I stepped off the escalator and scanned the crowd for my brother.

Josh laid a reassuring hand on the small of my back. "Don't worry, I'll know him. Look. There he is."

My eyes darted toward the direction Josh indicated and something deep inside me broke apart. A man was approaching us. He wore loose faded blue jeans, black leather shoes and a bulky, cream-colored fisherman's sweater.

Under normal circumstances, if I wasn't expecting to see Riley, this person would have walked right past me and I would never have known he was my brother. Today, however, I knew it was him. I felt the link between us, despite the fact that his looks had changed considerably.

The last time I saw him he was tall and disturbingly thin, and he wore a buzz cut with tattoos on his scalp. The man walking toward us was nothing like that at all. He had grown muscular over the years—he must have gained at least thirty pounds—and his dark hair was thick and wavy with traces of gray, which concealed the tattoos.

"Holly?" he asked.

"Yes."

"Wow." His expression warmed and I took note of the deep friendly laugh lines at the outer corners of his eyes. "Look at you. I can't believe it. The last time I saw you, you were what… thirteen?"

"I was."

He held out his arms and I eagerly stepped into them. "It's good to see you," he softly said. "I'm glad you wrote."

"Me, too," I replied as we stepped apart.

He turned to Josh. "And it's great to see you too, man." They shook hands. "How weird is this? After all these years…"

"Thanks for having us," Josh said.

Riley glanced back and forth between the two of us and wagged a finger. "So…are you guys a couple, or what?"

"No, we're just friends," I quickly explained. "We only reconnected a few days ago. Josh has been helping me out. Getting me through…a few rough patches."

Riley continued to stare at the two of us as if baffled by my explanation but he didn't seem to want to pry. Instead, he gestured toward the main doors. "My car's parked just outside. Do you have any bags to pick up or just your carry-ons?"

"Just these." I pulled my suitcase on its squeaky wheels. "Did your wife come with you?"

"No, Lois had to pick up the kids at pre-school, but she'll be home when we get back. She has dinner planned. Hope you like hamburgers."

"Love 'em," Josh said as we followed Riley to his car—a Nissan Sentra that looked as if it had seen better days. I suspected he'd picked it up secondhand.

As soon as we were on the road—a narrow, straight highway with a flat, endless open field to the right—we muddled through the usual small talk. Riley asked questions like: 'How was the flight?' 'So you're in med school now? That's amazing.' 'And you're a cop, Josh? What division?'

Before long, the small talk switched gears and took the inevitable turn.

"How's Leah?" Riley asked. "She must be what...in her third or fourth year of a residency by now? What did she end up choosing as a specialty?"

My lips fell open and a slow wave of dread surged through me. I glanced over my shoulder at Josh who was seated in the back. He shook his head with regret and gave me a sympathetic look.

"How long has it been since you've been in touch with anyone?" I carefully asked Riley.

"At least five years," he replied.

"That's a long time."

"Yeah." Riley kept one hand on the wheel and rubbed the back of his neck with the other. "Eventually there just came a point when Lois was at her wit's end with me. She insisted I stop trying to make contact. She wanted me to leave the past in the past and focus on the here and now."

"I see." My stomach began to churn. Of course, it had occurred to me that Riley might not even know about Leah's death, but this confirmed it.

"Would you mind pulling over for a minute?" I pointed to the side of the road. "We need to stop."

"Are you feeling okay?" Riley shot me a worried glance, then checked his rearview mirror and flicked the blinker. The wheels hit the gravel and it grew noisy in the car until the vehicle came to a halt.

Riley shifted into park and shut off the engine. Other cars zoomed past us.

Realizing I had no choice but to deliver devastating news to this man who was in many ways a stranger to me, I reached for the door handle. "Let's take a walk."

Riley hesitated before getting out of the car.

A strong wind gusted across a field where we got out. Riley came around the front of the car to meet me. Together we moved away from the shoulder of the road and walked toward a farmer's fence.

"I have some bad news," I said, pushing my windblown hair out of my eyes. "I'm sorry to be the one to have to tell you this."

His eyebrows drew downward in a frown. "That doesn't sound good."

"It's not," I replied, turning my back to the wind. "Just over two years ago, Leah was diagnosed with ALS."

Riley shoved his hands deep into his pockets. "You're joking."

"No. Unfortunately it progressed quickly and…" I looked down at my shoes. "I'm sorry, Riley. She passed away a few weeks ago."

A driver sped by on the road and honked his horn at another.

Solemnly lifting my gaze, I gave Riley a moment to take in what I'd just explained.

"No," he said, shaking his head in denial. "That can't be."

I didn't know what to say. The look of agony on his face broke my heart and took away my ability to form coherent sentences. A vein pulsed at his forehead. His eyes filled with tears and he turned away from me toward the distant horizon.

Abruptly, he walked off.

"Riley..." I made a move to follow but he held up a hand, as if to warn me to stay back.

I watched him walk along the edge of the fence until he was some distance away, then he stopped and bowed his head. He dropped to his knees, bent forward on his elbows and squeezed fistfuls of his hair while he rocked back and forth.

His despair caused a rise of emotion in me that was almost paralyzing.

Turning toward the car, I saw Josh get out. He shut the door, met my gaze and approached.

"I don't know what to do," I said helplessly while my head filled with aching, throbbing anguish.

"Just give him a minute," Josh replied as he squinted into the wind.

Finally, Riley sat back on his heels, then rose to his feet. He wiped his cheeks with the backs of his hands and turned to face us. I felt his pain and anger crash over me like a tsunami. I wanted to crawl under a rock and hide there.

Tramping heavily over the tangled, matted grass, he returned to where we stood waiting.

"Why didn't I know?" he asked. "Why didn't anyone tell me? It was *him*, wasn't it?"

"You mean Dad," I said.

He nodded. "He didn't let you call or write. My God, my sister was *dying*! Why didn't you just stand up to him and do it anyway?"

"Like *you* did?" I challenged.

"Damn right, like I did!"

Josh stood in silence, watching Riley with a dark and steady intensity.

"We didn't know where you were," I argued in my defense. "All this time, Mom thought you were either dead or rotting in jail somewhere—and not a single word from you to ease her mind or let her know you were okay. So please don't accuse me of not keeping in touch."

Riley shuddered and gritted his teeth as he spoke. "I wrote to you and I tried to call. Dad kept changing the number. He told me to stop. He said none of you wanted to hear from me. When I met Lois, I tried again, but he threatened me with a restraining order if I continued to write or if I tried to come home. I didn't want to go back to prison."

My breath caught in my throat. "I don't understand."

"He said I was causing you all great pain and suffering—that you still had nightmares about the night I broke into the house—and that I wasn't welcome."

"What about Facebook or something?" I asked. "You could have friended me."

"I'd given up by then," he explained, his tone growing quieter. "After a while, I had to because it was ripping me apart inside. It made everything so much harder."

I suspected he meant staying clean.

We all stood in silence for a long moment, breathing hard beneath the enormous overcast sky. Riley tilted his head back and looked up at the clouds. They rolled briskly by.

"I can't believe I didn't even know she was sick," he said, "and that Dad wouldn't lift the iron curtain—not even for that." He pulled his gaze from the sky and looked at me with a brotherly apology. "I'm sorry, Holly."

Tears blinded my eyes. "I'm sorry, too," I replied as I stepped into his open arms.

Josh and I promised to stay three days with Riley, Lois and their two children, Danny and Trudy. Josh slept on the sofa in the basement rec room while I took the upstairs guest room.

There was much to discuss about the future. Neither Riley nor I was certain how our mother would conduct herself when she learned what our father had done. Or maybe, deep down, she'd already known. Maybe she would continue to follow his rules for the rest of her life without ever challenging them. '*He's my husband*,' she'd always said, as if that explained everything.

Mostly, however, Riley and I reminisced about Leah and grieved for the tragic loss of her. We also filled in the blanks on all the missing years. After the children went to bed the first night, the four of us gathered around the kitchen table where Riley spoke of the darkest, most shocking moments of his life—the majority of which had taken place during his teen years and later in prison.

He also shared with us how he'd met Lois after an AA meeting not long after his release. "She was working in a nearby coffee shop," he said.

Lois gave him an affectionate smile. "I still remember what you were wearing that night—blue jeans and a U2 concert T-shirt." She turned to Josh and me to explain. "Your brother walked in and ordered a large green tea. I was so smitten, just from the way he smiled at me, that I messed up the order and gave him the wrong change."

"You gave me too much," Riley added.

"Yes, but you were honest and you pointed it out to me. I knew instantly that you were a decent guy."

Riley slanted her a look. "Until you found out I went to prison."

I noticed they were holding hands now, grinning at each other playfully.

"I still thought you were a good guy." Lois turned to us again. "He came in a couple of times a week for a whole year. I started asking for the evening shifts just to make sure I didn't miss seeing him. He'd always order green tea. And we'd talk."

Riley leaned back comfortably in his chair. "This one had a way of getting me to open up and confess everything. She calmed me down, made me feel like everything was going to be okay."

"How long was it before you started dating?" Josh asked.

"It was a year before I brought Riley home to meet my parents. Even after that, I waited a long time before I told them about his prison record. I wanted to make sure they knew him really well first."

"What did they say when you told them?" I asked.

Lois let out a slow breath. "Well, Holly…They didn't like it, but they'd grown attached to him by then and knew how much I loved him. Besides that, they raised me to believe that what is done is done and you can't change it, but the future doesn't have to be dictated by the past. All I wanted was to venture forward and start a life with this man."

"And that's one of the things I loved about you," Riley said to her, raising her hand to his lips and kissing the back of it. "What

I *still* love about you—that you had faith that even a man like me could change."

"With help," Lois clarified, turning her gaze back to Josh and me. "Riley runs an addictions support group at the church and he still goes to regular AA meetings. And when all is said and done, he's a wonderful father."

I felt a warm glow somewhere deep inside me as I smiled at my brother.

Josh and Riley then recollected some of their happier childhood memories and eventually spoke about the infamous Clipper Lake Hotel incident.

"Of all my experiences as a kid," Riley said, "that probably stands out as the most vivid."

"Me, too," Josh replied, "though I always regretted that day."

"Why?" I asked, laying my hand on Josh's forearm.

He turned to me. "Because I believed it was the reason your family moved out of the neighborhood—which felt like someone had ripped an organ out of my chest." We gazed at each other intently under the bright kitchen light.

Josh returned his attention to Riley. "Holly thinks you moved because your father wanted a bigger house, but I always blamed myself after he came home and found the cops in his driveway."

"*That's* not why we moved," Riley told us with a strange laugh, as if the truth were common knowledge. "We moved because my dad thought your dad had the hots for my mother."

Josh and I responded together. "*What?*"

Riley scooped up a handful of peanuts from the bowl in front of him. "Don't worry," he said. "Nothing ever happened. They didn't have an affair or anything. Dad was just incredibly jealous of your dad because he didn't like coming home to find some other guy from the neighborhood fixing our leaky faucet or unclogging our toilet." Riley pointed a finger at Josh and spoke with a hint of humor that accentuated the laugh lines around his eyes. "And your dad *was* a flirt. You know that, right?"

"It's why my mother divorced him," Josh replied. "But I didn't know he was putting the moves on your mom."

Riley shook his head. "He wasn't, but it didn't matter. Dad's a control freak with a temper. I doubt you even know about the time they brawled in our garage. Remember when your dad had the black eye?"

"He said he fell off the ladder cleaning the gutters," Josh recollected.

Riley shook his head. "Nope."

"So that's why your father hated me?" Josh asked. "Because he hated my dad?"

Riley shrugged. "You and your father did bear a striking resemblance. You had the same charm that he did, and you know how Mom always loved *you*. Wow, you must have been a heartbreaker in high school. Sorry I missed that." He smiled and pointed a warning finger at me. "Baby sister, you better be careful with this guy. Let me know if he treats you wrong and I'll take care of it. I know people."

I laughed and lay my head on Josh's shoulder. "That's completely unnecessary. He's been a perfect gentlemen."

"Since when?" Riley replied, and we all laughed and continued talking until the wee hours of the morning when it was time, at last, to go to bed.

⁓

After a day spent traveling across the country—meeting my ex-convict brother for the first time in a decade and telling him that

our sister had just passed away—it would have made sense for me
to fall asleep as soon as my head hit the pillow.

Such was not the case.

Instead, my brain exploded like fireworks with thoughts,
memories and images from my life—in particular the past week,
concerning my time with Josh and everything we'd been through.

I tossed and turned until finally, I gave up trying. Flinging
the covers aside, I rose from bed and tiptoed downstairs to
the kitchen, filled a glass with water at the sink, then turned
toward the door that led to the basement where Josh was
sleeping.

The mere sight of the door made me feel slightly breathless.

All my senses heightened.

Thoughts of him, so near, changed rapidly to a sense of long-
ing, and I knew I could not continue to resist the urge to go to
him.

Padding softly across the cold linoleum floor, I slowly opened
the door which creaked on squeaky hinges, and peered down into
the darkness. The steady sound of Josh's breathing traveled up the
stairs and reached my ears.

I felt even more wide awake. All I wanted was to be close to
him. Lie with him. Be held by him. But what about Paul? He
seemed a million miles and hours away. I simply couldn't think of
him. I couldn't even picture his face.

With light footsteps, I descended the carpeted stairs and
waited briefly for my eyes to adjust to the darkness. Eventually I
became aware of the silvery moonlight streaming in through the
small basement window. It was just enough to lead me to the sofa
where Josh was sleeping under a thick red comforter.

Not wanting to wake him, I sat down on the carpet and rested
my cheek on the edge of the sofa, next to his face. For a long while

I remained there with my eyes closed, my legs tucked under me, listening to the sound of his breathing.

Then I felt gentle fingers combing through my hair...

"Hi," he whispered.

"Hi," I replied with a smile.

"Couldn't sleep?" he asked.

I shook my head. "Too much to think about."

He lifted the comforter to invite me in. "Come and get warm."

I climbed in beside him and relished the sensation of his body heat all around me as we found a comfortable spooning position.

"I'm glad you came to my door that day," I whispered. "Even though you turned my life upside down."

"Most people would consider that a bad thing," he replied, his breath hot and moist in my ear.

"I'm still not sure it isn't. I don't know what's happening here, Josh." His bare chest was warm and solid against my back; I felt a tight clenching of desire deep and low in my belly. "I'm supposed to be with someone else."

He held me tighter, squeezing his strong body up against the back of mine. "Are you sure about that?" I heard the sound of him swallow behind me and felt another unfathomable rush of desire.

"I'm not sure about anything. Look where we are. In Montana with the brother I thought I'd lost forever."

"And the friend I never imagined I'd see again."

I turned my head to the side to nuzzle my cheek against his nose and lips. My emotions began to whirl. My heart was pounding and my head was spinning. "Life is strange, isn't it?"

"Yes," he replied, laying a kiss on my cheek. "I'm starting to believe every day is a miracle."

The lush heat of his mouth on my skin caused a flurry of response in every part of my body. I shivered from the pleasure of it.

Rolling to face him, I lay my open palms on his cheeks. "Thank you."

"For what?"

"For holding me."

I touched my lips lightly to his and felt a swell of passion rise up within me as he pulled me closer and deepened the kiss.

My night on the sofa with Josh was beyond anything I'd ever experienced or could have imagined. Of course I'd been with men before. I was twenty-five years old and had been in a serious committed relationship for over a year. My feelings for Josh, however, were like some sort of vibrating force that began deep in the pit of my belly and sizzled outward to the tips of my fingers and toes, to the very top of my head. A part of me wanted to fight against its power, while another part of me only wanted to fall into it, to let myself be swept away.

The sun was just coming up when I slipped quietly back upstairs. I felt mind-bogglingly euphoric, as if I were lifting off my feet in the hallway and floating up to the ceiling. The happiness was almost frightening; I hadn't believed I could feel anything like it—not for a very long time. Not after losing Leah.

Of course, as soon as I got into bed and allowed myself to think about Paul, I felt a guilt-ridden wave of remorse, but it was nothing compared to the flood of joyful emotion that had brought me to my knees during the night. I wanted Josh with a raging soulful desire that simply couldn't be ignored. I felt as if I were breaking apart and dissolving into a billion tiny particles— floating outward to a place where the real world didn't exist.

I shut my eyes and willed myself to wrestle my feelings under control. *Don't be such a romantic, Holly.*

In my mind I knew the real world did exist and I had to muddle through it. I had my future to think about—the practicalities of my family relationships, school, my career, money. I barely knew Josh. These were strange and difficult circumstances. I couldn't simply let my heart float away with him.

An hour later, I rose from bed when I heard Lois get up to make breakfast for the children.

Later, she and Riley took us all to the zoo where we wandered leisurely through peaceful, meandering wooded lanes to view the animal exhibits. Lois pushed Trudy in a stroller while Riley kept an eye on little Danny who enjoyed running ahead to see the wolverines, grizzlies and bighorn sheep.

All the while, there was an inescapable energy between Josh and me—like a hissing, crackling electric current. He felt it, too. I knew he did, and it drove me mad with a need to be alone with him, to talk this through—but mostly to touch him, step into his arms and run my open palms across his bare chest and broad shoulders. To feel his soft lips on my neck…

It was almost lunchtime when Josh paused on the path and grimaced slightly.

"Are you all right?" I asked. "I knew we shouldn't have walked so far."

"I'll be fine. I just need to sit down for a minute." He pointed. "I see a bench."

"Take your time," Lois said. "Why don't the two of you meet us at the picnic area in about a half hour? It's just across that bridge, past the bald eagle exhibit. We'll take the kids and go check out the river otters."

Lois pushed the stroller down the path while Josh and I sat down on the bench. He immediately took hold of my hand.

"How are you doing?" he asked. "Are you feeling all right today?"

I faced him and smiled. "Far better than all right. What about you?"

His eyes glimmered with a teasing intimacy that melted my resolve to remain practical. He lay a hand on his abdominal scar. "I'm good, too—though I might have overdone it a bit last night."

"I'm so sorry. That's *my* fault."

"Don't apologize, Holly. I'd do it again in a heartbeat. Right now, in fact, if we weren't in a public place."

I smiled. "So would I." Sitting back, I pondered the joy that flooded through me just from looking up at the treetops swaying gently in the breeze. "Although I've never cheated on anyone before," I added. "It's important that you know that."

"I know, and neither have I. It's strange. I was in Paul's position not that long ago and I was pretty bitter about it. I never imagined I'd be on the other side of things, but here I am, hoping and praying you're going to end it with him."

I shot him a look. "Is that what you want? You're sure about that?"

"Yes. Definitely. I want it today. Right now."

Though I was confused and vulnerable and terrified about rushing into something before testing the waters, I was relieved that he didn't hesitate. Not for a single fraction of a second.

"I don't see how I *can't* put an end to it," I replied. "Not after last night."

"Do you feel guilty?"

"Of course," I replied, "but it's not just that."

"What is it, then?"

I reached for Josh's hand. "I don't want to fight this. I can't explain it, but everything in my heart and mind is urging me to leap right in. Blindly. I can't possibly walk away from you. At the same time, the thought of telling Paul it's over is killing me. He's a decent guy. He did nothing wrong."

Josh wrapped his arm around my shoulder, pulled me close and kissed the top of my head. "When I woke up this morning I was afraid—afraid that you were going to tell me we made a mistake, and that I should go home and give you some space to decide what you really want."

"I don't want space," I replied. "Not from you. I'm just going to have to figure out how to make everything else work around what we've started. I have to say good-bye to Paul even though it's going to be hard. I don't love him—not like I should—and he deserves better."

A bluebird landed in a tree across from where we sat. For a long while I sat in Josh's arms, admiring the bird's vivid plumage until she lifted off the branch and flew away again.

Not long after Josh and I boarded the plane to return home to Boston, we ascended to a height just above the clouds. The sun was in the midst of setting and the sky was a magnificent, radiant shade of pale orange.

"It's so beautiful." I gazed out the window as the starboard wing dipped low to turn us in the direction of the east coast.

Josh clasped my hand and laid a kiss on my shoulder.

"It's like flying through heaven," I said.

Then all at once I had an epiphany, or maybe it was just pure reckless emotion. As I looked out over the world beneath the fiery sunset, everything suddenly made sense.

Turning away from the window, I wet my lips and spoke with conviction. "I don't want to live at home anymore, and I don't want to be a doctor either."

Josh regarded me intently. "Are you sure?"

"Yes. I still want to finish medical school, because I love the science of it, but when I'm done I want to do what you do—have a career in law enforcement, too. It's what I've wanted since I was thirteen. Maybe I could apply to the Boston Police or even the FBI and do forensics. There must be some options."

"Of course there are," he replied. "There are plenty of options for someone like you."

"Is that crazy?" I asked.

"No," he replied. "You should do what you love."

Together, we turned to the window again to watch the sun dip into the soft bed of clouds.

"I can't believe this is my life," I whispered. "It hardly seems real."

"I feel the same way," Josh replied, gathering me into his arms to settle in for the rest of the flight home.

At which time I would have to face my father.

I went to school the next day, worked hard to catch up on what I'd missed, and I texted my mother to let her know I'd be dropping by that night after dinner.

What I neglected to mention was that I intended to bring Josh and that by the time we got there, I would have broken up with Paul.

We pulled into the driveway shortly after 8:00 p.m. With a wave of apprehension, I looked up at the front of the house.

"My heart's pounding," I said. "This hasn't been an easy night. Maybe I should have spaced all this stuff out."

Earlier that evening, I'd spent half an hour on the phone with Paul, struggling to explain why I needed to put an end to our relationship—which wasn't easy because he'd done nothing wrong. Then I spent another half hour crying on the sofa.

Josh released the clasp on his seatbelt and squeezed my hand. "Everything will be fine."

A moment later we were climbing the steps. When we reached the porch, I briefly considered ringing the doorbell, but that seemed an odd thing to do since I still lived there, officially. So I dug into my purse for my keys, unlocked the door and walked in.

"Hello!" I called out.

We were greeted by a delicious aroma of freshly baked cookies.

"Smells good in here," Josh whispered.

The lights were on in the kitchen but the rest of the house was dark and quiet...until I heard Mom's voice at the top of the stairs.

"Is that you, Holly?" She quickly descended. As she hurried toward me, she glanced briefly at Josh and threw her arms around my shoulders, pulling me close. "I'm so happy to see you."

"Me, too." I let her hold me as long as she needed to, then we stepped apart and I gestured to Josh. "You remember Josh Wallace?"

"Of course." Her expression warmed. "Good heavens, look at you. All grown up. A police officer I hear. Where has the time gone?"

"Hi, Mrs. James." He gave my mother a dazzling, heartfelt smile that, despite the hardships of the evening, melted me into a giant puddle of happy infatuation.

To my surprise, Mom held out her arms and hugged him, too. Then she led us into the kitchen for cookies.

"How's your mother?" she asked Josh.

"Very well," he replied. "She remarried last year."

"Lovely. So she's happy, I presume?"

"Very. She married a good man."

"That's wonderful," Mom said. "Will you tell her I said hello?"

"Of course."

We sat down on the stools at the center island where the cookies were displayed on a three-tiered, sterling silver serving dish. Mom moved to the fridge to withdraw a carton of milk.

"Is Dad here?" I cautiously asked.

She poured us each a glass and shook her head. "He wanted to be, but he had a surgery this evening. He said it might run late."

"Ah." I was both relieved and disappointed because I'd been dreading this confrontation, yet at the same time I wanted to get it over with. I wanted to tell both my parents that I was no longer with Paul—I was with Josh now—and that we had just visited Riley in Montana. Most importantly, I wanted them to understand what sort of future I saw for myself.

Since Dad wasn't there, I decided to confide in my mother, regardless.

"You're probably wondering where I've been for the past few days," I said.

"I can guess," she replied, lifting an eyebrow from where she stood on the opposite side of the island. "Your father wasn't too happy when he saw your car parked in front of Josh's house. No offense, Josh."

"None taken."

I let out a breath of frustration. "He banged pretty hard at the door but we didn't answer. He seemed too angry."

"I can't say I blame you for not answering," she replied. "And Josh, I apologize if his behavior was disrespectful in any way."

Surprised by her candor, I wondered if she would have said something like that if Dad had been standing there beside her. Probably not. Knowing the dynamic of their relationship as well as I did, I suspected she would have remained silent through most of this conversation.

"No worries," Josh said.

I reached for a cookie, set it on my plate but found I didn't have much of an appetite, so I simply leaned forward on my elbows.

"We weren't at Josh's house the whole time," I began to explain.

"Oh?"

"That's what I came here to talk to you about," I continued. "A few nights ago I sent an email to Riley. He said he wanted to see me, so Josh and I hopped on a flight to Montana to pay him a visit."

Mom stood motionless, blinking. "You *saw* him."

I nodded my head.

"How was he?"

"Great," I eagerly replied. "He was happy and looked terrific. He lives in a good neighborhood. His wife is very nice and his children are adorable. He's okay, Mom. You don't need to worry about him. You'd be proud. He's really turned his life around. "

Her cheeks flushed red and she raised a hand to her mouth. "Thank God," she whispered, turning her back on us.

Quickly, I rose from my stool to circle around the island and embrace her. "He'd love to hear from you," I gently added. "He said he tried contacting us a number of times over the years but Dad always told him to stay away and he even threatened him with a restraining order. But that has to stop, Mom. We can't go on like that. Dad shouldn't be able to keep us apart. I fully intend to see Riley again, whether Dad likes it or not."

Just then, the front door opened. My mother gasped and quickly wiped the tears from her face, as if to hide them.

Anger poured through me at the fact that both of us were so unsettled by my father's arrival. How had it come to this? How had he gained so much power over everyone? It wasn't as if he beat us. That sort of thing had been reserved for Riley.

Maybe it was because we'd witnessed it. We knew what he was capable of.

Or maybe it was the money. He could cut me off if he wanted to. Was that it?

Hearing the sound of his footsteps approaching from the front hall, I clenched my jaw and met Josh's steady gaze.

My father walked into the kitchen and regarded each of us individually. Josh slowly stood up.

For a tense moment, I wasn't sure what was going to happen. A part of me thought—and hoped—maybe my father might surprise us all, stroll forward to shake Josh's hand and say, "Nice to see you. Welcome." He could certainly be charming when he wanted to be. I'd seen it many times. *Most* of the time, in fact.

His eyes met mine. "We were worried about you," he said.

"You didn't need to be," I replied. "I texted Mom and told her I was okay. That I was staying with a friend."

He turned to Josh. "And you're the friend, I assume."

"That's right," Josh calmly replied.

A sharp feeling of agitation rose up in my throat.

"How do you think Paul would feel about this?" my father asked me.

"It's not really any of his business anymore," I explained, "because I ended our relationship a few hours ago."

Dad closed his eyes briefly, then gestured toward Josh. "Because of this guy."

"Yes," I admitted, denying nothing, making no apologies.

My father's head drew back as if I had swung a wooden plank in front of his face. "What are you saying? That you want to be with this man here?" He pointed at Josh, who exercised remarkable self-control by remaining silent. "Is that it?"

"Please stop talking about him like he's not here." I moved around the kitchen island to stand before my father, who was a full twelve inches taller than me. "We came here tonight to tell you that I'm moving out. I'll be looking for my own apartment, but in the meantime I'll be staying with Josh. And yes, we're involved. In fact, we just got back from a trip to Montana where we visited Riley for three days. And guess what? Josh stayed in my room. We slept in the same bed."

"Holly!" my mother scolded.

Maybe I was more like my brother than anyone realized—myself especially—because I had no regrets about what I'd just said. In fact, I *wanted* to rouse my father's anger. I *wanted* to provoke him.

Dad regarded me like a bull about to charge. I was prepared to drop into a karate stance if I had to, but to my surprise, he balled his hand into a fist and swung a punch at Josh.

Before I could shout at him to stop, Josh had grabbed him by the shoulder, twisted his arm and dropped him firmly, face down, on the floor. He continued to restrain my father with a knee to the spine, arm leveraged, a tight grip around his wrist.

I knew Josh could dislocate my father's shoulder in an instant if he were so inclined.

"Are you all right, sir?" Josh calmly asked.

"No, dammit!" Dad shouted indignantly, but it was his ego that was bruised, not his body.

"I'm going to back off now." Josh let go of Dad's wrist, rose to his feet and took two steps away. Grimacing with pain, he lay a hand on his abdomen over the incision and bent forward slightly.

"Are you all right?" I asked.

He nodded, but bit down hard on his lower lip as he leaned on the center island.

Mom watched the scene in silent horror, both hands covering her face.

"I'm sorry," I said to her. "I didn't want it to be like this."

Dad rose awkwardly to his feet. "I told you not to contact Riley!" he shouted at me.

"Really Dad? That's all you have to say right now?"

He scowled and took a deep breath. "Mark my words, if you walk out of here with that man…" He pointed a threatening finger at Josh. "Don't expect to ever come back. That's not how it works in this house."

"No?" I said. "That's not how the great machine operates? Did I push the wrong button?"

With a shake of my head, I turned to hug my mother and whispered in her ear: "Please call me. I'll text you my new address. You can visit."

Deeply concerned about Josh's condition, I took hold of his hand and left the kitchen. "I hope you didn't tear anything," I said quietly as we crossed the hall.

"I'm fine," he replied. "Sorry about that."

"Don't apologize. You were perfect. And you're not fine. I'm going to check that incision as soon as we get in the car—and I'll be driving."

We grabbed our coats and walked out.

"You don't have to look for your own place, you know," he mentioned as we descended the stairs. He moved awkwardly, clearly in pain. "You can stay with me as long as you like. Rent free."

"I may need to take you up on that." I stayed with him on the stairs in case he might suddenly pass out. We reached his car and I took the keys from him. "Because nothing would give me greater pleasure than to drive my father completely stark raving mad."

"Who knew you were such a rebel?" Josh asked with an attractive, devilish grin as he got in on the passenger side.

"Certainly not me."

As soon as we were seated, I reached up and flicked on the interior light. "Lower your seat back."

He did as I asked and allowed me to open his jacket, lift his shirt and inspect the incision. "It's not bleeding," I said. "It looks all right." My eyes lifted to find him perspiring heavily. "What about your leg?"

"Hurts like hell."

I glanced down at his thigh. "There's no blood on your jeans so that's a good sign. I'll check it as soon as we get home. And you shouldn't have done that."

There was a look of raw determination on his face. "I didn't even realize I was doing it until he hit the floor."

I couldn't help but smile. "I know that feeling."

A moment later we were pulling out of the driveway. I didn't let myself look back.

Breaking Open

Josh Wallace

Nearly two weeks after our confrontation with Holly's parents, I had the dream again.

I was driving through the rain, alone in my patrol car, wipers beating back and forth, lights flashing. As I rounded a sharp curve, a woman pushed a baby carriage out in front of me.

I slammed a foot on the brake pedal. My tires skidded over the shiny pavement. Whack! *I hit the carriage. It flew into the air.*

The baby, swaddled in a white blanket, bounced like a football over the hood of my car and smashed the windshield. I watched everything as if it were happening in slow motion, then squinted to try and refocus my eyes on the road.

I was still traveling at full speed.

Leah!

She stood on the center line, feet braced apart, both hands splayed out in front of her.

"Stop!" She mouthed the words: "Go back!" *Then she vanished before connecting with my grill.*

I pulled the car to a screeching halt, looked over my shoulder to see the mother on her knees at the side of the road, reaching for her baby.

I shifted into reverse to help them.

"No!"

I sat bolt upright in bed.

It took me a moment to understand where I was. Holly was rubbing my back, stroking her fingers through my sweat-drenched hair, speaking urgently.

"It was just a dream, Josh. You're fine. Everything's okay."

My heart pummeled my ribcage as I lay back down. She kissed my forehead, then wrapped her arm around me and snuggled close.

I shut my eyes and tried to go back to sleep, but it was no use. I had to get up.

Over the next few weeks, Holly secured herself a line of credit at the bank and found a small furnished bachelor apartment not far from the university. I was sorry to see her leave and insisted she could stay with me as long as she liked, but she was determined to get her own place and live independently for a while.

We continued to talk on the phone every night and spent time together on the weekends, and she maintained contact with her mother through regular texts and phone calls. Mrs. James admitted that she had called Riley and fully intended to visit him, but she was keeping it secret from her husband until she figured out how to manage it—and *him*.

"Get this," Holly said to me when I met her for lunch at the hospital after one of my physio appointments. "Mom's been seeing a therapist ever since Leah was first diagnosed. I didn't know until she told me this morning. She's been trying to get Dad to go for counseling, too, but he won't do it."

"Why doesn't that surprise me?" I asked as I dug into my salad.

"It doesn't surprise me either," Holly replied, "but I wish he'd budge on something. *Anything.* Even just to show us that he's not made of stone."

"Maybe your mom will be able to talk him into it after every-thing that's happened lately," I suggested.

I would have liked to hold out hope for that, but I think deep down, neither of us truly believed it would happen.

⟿

When the time came for me to return to work, I was beyond ready. My wounds had healed well and I felt fit and strong—though I knew I'd be kidding myself if I thought I could chase after a perp and leap over a chain link fence anytime soon.

As a result, my lieutenants assigned me to a desk job until they deemed me fit for regular duty. I saw a department-appointed therapist twice a week, always in the mornings. Who knows? Maybe they felt those bullets I took should count as a free ticket out of the graveyard shift. I told them I could handle anything, but they were determined to ease me slowly and gradually back into the patrol car.

The therapist asked me all sorts of questions about my thoughts and feelings since my return to work and I answered everything honestly, though I never made any reference to what happened to me during my stay in the hospital. I said nothing about how I floated to the ceiling in the operating room, or how I spoke to Leah—a dead person—nor did I draw any attention to the fact that my in-hospital psychiatric appointments had been mysteriously cancelled.

The last thing I needed was a note in my chart saying "patient suffers from severe hallucinations and deliriums."

I did my best to put it behind me, but it was hard to forget.

⟿

I was just finishing my shift on a Wednesday when a panicked text came in from Holly.

Josh...You there? Please answer...

I quickly typed a reply: *I'm here. Call me.*

Within ten seconds, my phone rang. I quickly swiped the screen to answer it. "Hey," I said, raising it to my ear. "What's up?"

She spoke quickly in a strained voice. "Mom just called me. She said she and Dad had a huge argument and she's locked herself in her bedroom. She wants to leave but she doesn't know if he'll let her. I'm worried. She was whispering the whole time."

"Did he hit her?" I asked. "Was there any sort of physical altercation?"

"No, but she said she doesn't feel safe. She's afraid to come out of her room. She asked me to come and get her but I don't have my car here. Can you go?"

I grabbed my keys off the desk and headed out. "I'm on my way right now."

Fifty-two

≈⟨⟩≈

Still in uniform, I pulled into Dr. James's driveway, quickly got out of the car, ran up the steps and rang the doorbell. When no one answered, I banged five times with the edge of my fist. "Dr. James! Are you home?"

His car was in the driveway and there were lights on inside. I listened carefully for voices but heard nothing until the sound of footsteps approached. At last the door opened.

Dr. James, dressed in jeans and a navy golf shirt, greeted me with a frown. "What are *you* doing here?" His gaze raked disapprovingly from the brim of my police hat to the badge pinned on my shirt, then down to my gun belt and black boots.

"Your wife called Holly and asked to be picked up. Holly couldn't leave the hospital so she asked me to come instead."

"My wife doesn't need a ride anywhere," Dr. James replied.

I carefully scrutinized his expression, searching for signs of duplicity or agitation, and noticed his right hand flexing and fisting. "Where is your wife, sir?"

"She's upstairs."

"Could you ask her to come down please? I'd like to speak to her."

Dr. James glared at me intensely. "This isn't any of your business, Josh."

"Well, since your daughter asked me to stop by and check on her mother, I think that makes it very much my business. Mind if I come in?"

His brow furrowed. "Yes, I do mind."

I held his gaze steadily in mine. "Let's not make this any more difficult than it has to be. I need to see Mrs. James. She called for assistance and said she didn't feel safe. If we can just clear that up, I'll get out of your way."

Though I was still standing on the porch with the screen door between us, I caught sight of something over the doctor's shoulder. It was Mrs. James descending the stairs with a suitcase.

Dr. James turned around. "Where are you going?" he asked her.

She set the suitcase down in the wide foyer and went to fetch a coat off a hook in the back hall. "I'm leaving."

Dr. James strode toward her. I immediately pulled the screen door open and stepped inside.

"No, you're not," he harshly said. "You can't leave."

Mrs. James donned her coat and began to button it. "Yes, I can. It's my choice and I'm leaving with Josh."

"But we're not done talking about this."

"We've been talking about it for weeks, Robert," she said. "Years, in fact." She picked up her suitcase and started walking toward me at the door. "You know I want us both to visit Riley, but you won't even consider it. It's not fair. We always do what *you* want us to do, but you never bend an inch for us. It's your way or the highway. And today I'm taking the highway."

"Margie, wait…"

"And I've asked you a thousand times to come to therapy with me, but you won't do that either."

He followed her to the door. "I don't need a therapist."

She stopped and whirled around. "So you've said. But I think you need it more than anyone. I'm just in therapy to help me figure out how to cope with *you*!"

He grabbed hold of her arm but she roughly shook him off. "Don't touch me, Robert!"

He blinked at her in shock as she turned and followed me out the front door and down the steps. We walked quickly to my car and got in.

"Are you all right?" I asked.

Her hands were shaking uncontrollably as she tried to buckle her seatbelt. "Yes. Thank you for coming to get me."

"It was no problem." I waited until she was buckled in before I backed out. "Do you know where you want to go? Do you have friends or family you'd like to call, besides Holly?"

"My family lives in New York," she replied. "I was thinking I might go to a hotel for tonight."

"You don't have to do that." I glanced in the rearview mirror. Dr. James was watching us from outside on the covered veranda as we pulled away. "You can stay at my place until Holly gets home. Then I'll take you over there."

She closed her eyes and let her head fall back on the headrest. "Thank you, Josh. That's very kind of you."

As I drove out of the neighborhood, I glanced at her with concern. "Are you sure you're all right? He didn't hurt you, did he?"

She lifted her head and looked at me. "No. That's at least one thing I can honestly say: He's never laid a violent hand on me. But I've seen him do it to others, you and Riley included, so I've never felt a hundred percent confident that he wouldn't eventually lose his temper with me." She gazed out the window. "He was pretty angry today. We've never fought like that before. It was partly my fault, I suppose, because I didn't back down this time, but if I had to do it all again, I wouldn't change a thing. I just wish he had agreed to see Riley. Or at least to go and talk to someone about all this."

I gave her a moment to collect herself. "You can stay with me as long as you need to, Mrs. James."

"Thank you, Josh," she said, looking straight ahead, "but I'll be booking a flight to Montana this evening and leaving the city as soon as I can. I don't know what it'll mean for my marriage, but surprisingly, I don't really care. All I want to do is see my son."

The Holiday Season

Josh Wallace

Two weeks before Thanksgiving, I arrived home to a telephone message from Riley which included an invitation for Holly and me to join him and his family for the long holiday weekend. It wasn't easy to tell my own mother that we wouldn't be coming to her place after all, but she understood when I explained the situation. My sister Marie would be there with her husband and kids, so she wouldn't be alone. And we promised we'd come for leftovers the day after we returned.

On Thursday evening, Holly and I boarded a plane and flew to Billings for what turned out to be an intimate and emotional family gathering with Mrs. James, who had been staying with Riley and Lois since the day she left Boston. There were tears and laughter, endless conversations about the past and future—and of course delicious Thanksgiving fare…a slow-roasted turkey dinner with all the trimmings, giant servings of carrot cake, pumpkin pie and ice cream, and indulgent hours spent in front of the television watching the Macy's Thanksgiving Day Parade.

Later in the day, while everyone was stretched out on the sofa digesting the meal, I smelled coffee brewing, so I went into the kitchen to find Mrs. James scrubbing a pot at the sink.

Grabbing a dish towel, I took the pot from her to dry it before she had a chance to set it in the rack.

"Thanks Josh," she said with a smile as she emptied the water out of the sink, then removed her yellow rubber gloves and set them on the counter.

When I finished drying the pot, she asked if I'd like a cup of coffee.

"I'd love one," I replied.

She withdrew two mugs from the cupboard. "You and Holly seem to be getting along well," she said as she poured.

"Better than well," I replied. "I can't imagine what my life would be like right now if I hadn't met her."

Mrs. James grinned at me, and the memory of those kind eyes from my boyhood made everything feel perfectly right... exactly as it was meant to be.

Well, *almost*....

"Those are nice words, Josh," she said. "I'm glad you're happy."

Leaning against the counter, I crossed one ankle over the other, glanced over my shoulder to listen for the others, and lowered my voice. "For the most part we are, but I have to be honest, Mrs. James. I'm having some trouble dealing with the way things have turned out."

She inclined her head. "How so?"

I paused. "I'm a family man—you know that. My mom and stepdad are everything to me, and you were like a second mother to me when I was kid. Riley and Leah were like family to me, too, and it's killing me to think that I might have played a part in the problems between you and your husband. I know I'm not your husband's favorite person in the world, and maybe if it weren't for me, you would never have moved from Sycamore Street. But it seems that ever since the day I walked through your door, your whole world has been exploding."

"In a *good* way," she said. "And it's hardly your fault that I've left my husband. That's been building for years."

I looked down at my shoes and nodded. "I just don't want Holly to lose her family. She hasn't spoken to her father since the night he and I got into a scuffle in your kitchen."

Mrs. James sat down at the table. "You know, I thought after she stood up to him and walked out, Robert might finally see the light and stop being such a hard-liner, but he didn't. He just *couldn't.*"

I swirled the coffee around in my cup. "I'm sorry to hear that, because the main reason I came in here to talk to you was to tell you that…" I paused for a moment and lowered my voice even further. "I know this might seem a bit sudden, but I want to marry Holly someday." Mrs. James sat up straighter in her chair. "I haven't proposed or anything. She needs to finish school and I don't want to rush into anything, but when that day comes, I'd like to ask both you and your husband for your blessings. I just don't know if I'll ever get that from him. I'll accept it if I have to, but there must be some hope with you. And if Holly says yes to becoming my wife, I want her to know that she'll have family with her on her wedding day, that at least you'll be there to help her pick out a dress and someone will be able to walk her down the aisle."

Mrs. James smiled. "Josh Wallace, if you get down on one knee to propose to my daughter—if and when that happens—you can be sure I'll be there for dress fittings and helping her choose flower arrangements and whatever else she needs. I couldn't be happier to hear this, Josh, because I know you're a good man. I've always known it—even when you were little and you came into my kitchen to ask for popsicles in the summer.

"Back then I thought maybe one day you and Leah might end up together, but now that she's gone and you're with Holly, nothing could be more perfect. I still remember how you held her in that rocking chair when she was born. Something in me fell in love with you that day and I wished you could have been a second son to me, too. Now—if she gives you the answer you want—you *will* be, and I can't imagine a more wonderful gift of hope for Christmas. So there. You have my blessing ten times over. How's that?"

I swallowed hard over a dense lump in my throat. "It's pretty darn good, Mrs. James."

She rose to her feet. "And I think it's time you started calling me Margie," she said with a smile as she held out her arms.

I t was not a nightmare that woke me one cold December night when a blizzard raged outside my bedroom window. I felt no fear or panic when my eyes fluttered open. The dream was, to the contrary, strangely comforting.

A young and happy Leah ran through a field of dandelions on a hot summer evening. The summer season was coming to an end, however, and the bright yellow wildflowers had turned to seed. They floated upwards through the air like twinkling snowflakes as she ran toward the setting sun. I was tempted to follow, but I knew she didn't want me to. She just wanted me to watch her run to the other side.

I woke up, rose from bed and looked out at the storm.

"Do you ever dream about Leah?" I asked Holly the following night as we spoke on the phone, each of us lying in our beds.

"Sometimes," she replied. "It's usually something out of the past, like getting up for school and eating breakfast with her at the table in the old kitchen before the remodel. She was twelve years older than me. In many ways she was more like a mother than a sister."

"What was the kitchen like?" I asked, feeling curious about so many things.

"It was horrible," Holly replied with a grin. "The countertop was an ugly shade of green and there was wallpaper on the walls with bright yellow flowers."

I tried to imagine it. "What else do you dream about?"

"Concerning Leah?" She paused. "I don't know…There were some nightmares before she died. I once dreamed she was locked in a cage in our attic, screaming at me to let her out. At the time I thought it was because of her illness. She was essentially locked in her body and couldn't communicate or do anything for herself. That was difficult. Or maybe that had some connection to Riley being in prison. Who knows?"

Holly told me more about the hardships her family had endured during the last few months of Leah's life—which ended with a desperate rush to the hospital when she developed pneumonia in her final days.

"I wish you were here right now," I said before we hung up.

"Me, too," Holly replied. "Remind me…Why did I get this apartment again?"

I chuckled. "Because you wanted to be independent."

"Oh yeah, that." She sighed into the phone.

Sometime during the night, I dreamed of the kitchen Holly had described—with the green countertops and bright yellow wallpaper.

Leah sat at the table drinking a glass of milk, then she stood and wandered aimlessly through the house and into the front parlor.

The house was quiet. Empty and dark.

A Christmas tree, without decorations or gifts, stood in front of the window. She sat down on the floor in front of it and wept.

A s Christmas approached, I couldn't seem to shake the overwhelming urge to drive past the James' household on a
regular basis. Sometimes I would drive by in the mornings
on the way to work. Other times I checked on the house in the
evenings when the street was lit up with colorful outdoor lights
and life-size models of Santa Clause in his sleigh.

There was nothing festive, however, about the big red
Victorian set back from the road. It looked as if no one had lived
there in months. The front veranda hadn't been shoveled since the
blizzard, but there were fresh tire marks in the snow each morning, which suggested that Dr. James was still coming and going
from the hospital.

I drove by late one night and saw his car parked out front.
In an upstairs window, a television cast an eerie, flickering glow.

I drove home, called Holly to tell her what I had seen, and
suggested we at least send her father a Christmas card.

"Yes," she said without hesitation. "We should. Why don't we pop
by tomorrow night? I'll bring some sugar cookies and a poinsettia."

I agreed it was the right thing to do, and I hoped we'd be
given a better reception than last time.

ᴄ◦

Knowing it was rare for Holly's father to arrive home from work before 7:00 p.m., we showed up at 8:00. Unfortunately, the house was dark and his car wasn't in the driveway.

"We probably should have called," Holly said with disappointment as she shifted the big, red leafy plant on her lap. "But I was afraid he'd tell us not to come. Let's go inside anyway. I still have my keys. We can drop this off in the kitchen and leave the card. You take the plant. I'll take the cookies."

I unbuckled my seatbelt, took the plant out of her hands and carried it to the front walk.

"What a gorgeous night," she said, stopping to look up at the stars. "It's so quiet. There's not a single breath of wind."

I looked up as well and inhaled the fresh wintry air.

"It's so romantic," she added. "Honestly, I've never felt so happy."

"Even though things haven't turned out so well with your father?" I asked.

She pulled her gaze from the stars to look at me. "I remain ever hopeful. Maybe the cookies will make a difference."

"They are delicious," I replied with a grin. Then I took note of the snow-covered veranda. "Why don't you wait here for a minute while I clear off the steps?"

I set down the plant, returned to the car to grab the shovel out of my trunk and quickly established a path to the front door. She found the right key and we kicked the snow off our boots before letting ourselves in.

"It's freezing in here," she said, shivering as she switched on a light.

We removed our boots and coats. While I carried the poinsettia into the kitchen, she went to crank up the heat on the register.

Looking around, I noticed that even with Margie gone, everything was still tidy and spotless. There wasn't a single dirty dish in the sink or a jacket left draped over the back of a chair. No slippers that someone might have kicked off under the table.

It was disconcertingly quiet.

Holly appeared and set the cookies on the counter. "There's no Christmas tree," she said. "No decorations anywhere. Mom always took care of that stuff and made Christmas so beautiful. It seems very lonely."

"What do you want to do?" I asked.

"I don't know. There's an artificial tree in the attic. That's where all the decorations are. We could set it up."

"How do you think your father would feel about that?"

Holly sighed. "I have no idea. He's always been such a mystery to me." She thought about it for a few seconds, then turned to me. "I wonder what Leah would do in this situation."

I immediately thought of my dream. "I'm pretty sure she would want us to set up the tree."

"I think so too," Holly replied. "Let's get to it then. I'll make us some hot chocolate."

I kissed her on the cheek and asked for directions to the attic.

By 11:00, the tree was set up and decorated in the front parlor.

"It's lovely," Holly said, stepping back to admire our work. "I'm going to take a picture." She went to get her phone out of her purse, returned and snapped a photo. "Maybe I'll send this to Mom."

"The only thing that's missing are gifts under it," I said.

"You're right." She lowered her phone to her side. "It's kind of sad."

"We could come back tomorrow and bring something," I suggested.

"Yes. Maybe." She checked her watch. "It's late. Dad could be working all night for all we know. We should probably go."

Without another word, we made sure to turn off all the lights in the house—even the ones on the Christmas tree—gathered up our belongings and left.

As we drove home through the brightly lit city, we talked about our plans for Christmas Eve and Christmas Day, which included dinners with my family. Since it was late and we were tired, but neither of us wanted to say goodnight, Holly agreed to stay over at my place.

We also decided we'd make another attempt to visit Holly's father. *When* was the only question? We were still discussing options when there was a sudden urgent knock at the door.

Fifty-six

cc⁓ɔɔ

"It's your father," I said to Holly as I peered out the front window. "He's double parked again."

Holly, dressed in pink silk pyjamas, fuzzy slippers and a fleecy red Santa Clause robe she left here in a drawer, rose up on her tiptoes to look over my shoulder. "Do you think he's angry? Maybe he didn't want a Christmas tree this year."

"I don't know but I think we should answer it."

She agreed and followed me down the stairs.

We opened the door to find Dr. James standing stiffly in a tailored black overcoat and blood-red scarf. He held a Christmas box in his gloved hands.

"Hi, Dad," Holly said hesitantly.

"Hello," he replied, his breath visible on the chilly winter air. "I know it's late, but I noticed your lights were on."

I cleared my throat and opened the door wider. "It's no problem. We were up. Would you like to come in?"

Looking distinctly ill at ease, he nodded, stepped inside and followed us up the stairs.

"Can I get you anything, Dr. James?" I asked. "Coffee? A soda? Scotch?"

He didn't look at me. "A Scotch please, Josh. Thank you."

So far, it was the most civil conversation I'd ever had with the man. I wondered if I'd been dropped into the *Twilight Zone*. I'd certainly landed in stranger places.

"As long as you don't mind the cheap stuff." I went to the kitchen to fetch a bottle from the cupboard over the stove, while Holly took her father's coat and scarf and invited him into the living room to sit on the sofa.

I poured Scotch on the rocks for all three of us and carried them in.

"Thanks," Dr. James said.

"You must have worked late tonight?" Holly asked, glancing curiously at the Christmas box he'd set on the coffee table.

"Yes." He took a deep swig of the Scotch. "I came home and saw the cookies and poinsettia in the kitchen, and what you did in the parlor. That was very...*kind* of you."

I suspected it took a lot for him to cough up that word.

Holly tucked her legs up under her. "I hope you didn't mind. I still had a key so I let myself in. Then we thought the house seemed too quiet. It needed a little Christmas spirit."

"It did," he replied, never quite meeting her gaze.

I found myself letting out a slow breath as I leaned back in the leather chair.

"It has definitely been very quiet at the house," he explained, taking another gulp of Scotch and finally setting the glass down on the table. "I still can't believe your mother's gone. Sometimes I come home from the hospital and I imagine that she's come back. I can smell her perfume or I think I smell cookies, but she's never there. It's um..." He paused. "It's been unsettling to say the least. Especially now, at Christmas. She always made everything so special."

I said nothing while Holly touched her father's knee. "I'm sorry it turned out this way, Dad. It's not what I wanted."

He lifted an eyebrow and looked down at the floor. "Either way, you can't deny I had this coming."

"How do you mean?"

Of course Holly knew exactly what her father was referring to, but I understood that she wanted to hear it from *him*.

Dr. James twisted his wedding ring around on his finger. "You know I wasn't the easiest father in the world. I demanded a lot. Riley had it the worst."

"It was hard sometimes," she gently said.

He shut his eyes, cupped his forehead in a hand and shook his head. "I know. I've been talking to someone," he admitted. "Your mother was after me to do that for years and...Well, after she left..."

"Do you mean a therapist?" Holly asked.

He nodded. "I'm starting to realize that I've needed structure and rules in the house because I want to avoid the sort of conditions I grew up in. It was basically pure chaos."

Holly and I remained quiet and her father continued.

"There were days when my father used to come home drunk, take one look around at the mess and the noise with a wife and nine kids all living in a rundown shack, and he'd fly into a rage. My poor mother couldn't keep up with all the housework and we did our best to help out, but it was never enough."

He picked up his drink and held it in his hands.

"You didn't want to be like him," Holly said. "That's why you set all those rules—so that you would never come home to chaos."

Dr. James's Adam's apple bobbed as he swallowed. "But I *was* like him...at least with Riley. What was I thinking? To believe you can avoid chaos where children are concerned, and Lord knows, Riley was a handful. He was always strong willed, even as a toddler. He constantly tried to push me and test me. For a long time I thought he was put here on this earth just to bring me down. The harder I'd fight against it, try to keep things in order, the more like my father I became." He gritted his teeth and took another swig of Scotch.

"Is that why you wanted Riley to stay away?" Holly asked. "Did you think you'd become like that again if he came home?"

Dr. James nodded. "But obviously, my preferred solution to the problem didn't work out too well, because everybody's gone." The ice cubes clinked in his glass as he jiggled it and took the last sip. "All I wanted to do was make it through Christmas without torturing myself over all the stupid things I've said and done over the years. I've been trying to ignore the festivities mostly. I thought I could make it to January and just get on with life, but then I came home tonight and saw the tree all lit up in the parlor. It was one of those moments that shakes you. I felt like the Grinch when he heard the Whos singing down in Whoville. Remember that?"

Holly nodded and gave me a look, as if she was surprised that *he* remembered.

"Then I couldn't help myself," he continued. "I went upstairs to your room—just to look at all your books, medals and trophies and stuffed animals in all those baskets. Not much has changed in there since you were in high school." He pointed at the box on the table. "Then I saw *that* sitting on your bedspread, and it was like a giant light bulb flashed in my head."

Holly stared at the box. "I don't understand." She leaned forward, flung the lid aside, and pulled out the tissue paper. "Oh…"

"It's Oliver," Dr. James explained.

She held up a stuffed green bunny.

Shock erupted in my chest. I, too, sat forward in my chair.

Suddenly I was traveling again, into that dark tunnel toward the incredible light on the other side, to the place where I had recently relived the memory of the day in the hospital when I sat holding Holly in the rocking chair.

Leah reached for the gift on the floor at my feet…the gift for the baby.

"It's a bunny," she said, lifting the toy out of the bag. "Look, Mom." She carried it to her mother so she could feel how soft it was, then returned to my side. "She's going to love it."

The bunny in front of me this evening had changed a great deal. No longer fluffy and new, his color was faded. He was missing some stuffing and his head flopped to one side. Clearly this toy had been well loved.

"You still have him," I said with disbelief.

"I've had him forever," Holly replied. Then she cocked her head to the side. "But what do you mean?"

I couldn't speak for some reason.

Thankfully, Dr. James helped me out. "Josh gave you Oliver. He brought him to the hospital on the day you were born."

Holly's voice rose in surprise. "*You* gave me Oliver?"

All I could do was nod my head.

"No one ever told me that," Holly said. "Or maybe they did but I was too young to remember and I wouldn't have known who you were anyway." Holly turned to her father. "Why did you bring this?"

"Because I wanted you to know that I understand you're not a child anymore and I need to let you live your own life and be with whoever you want to be with. Maybe it's Josh. All I know is…as soon as I picked up that fluffy old bunny and remembered how you used to squeeze him when you were scared, I had to come over here. I had to see you."

Holly wrapped her arms around her father's shoulders. "I'm glad you did. Thank you, Dad. This means a lot to me." She drew back and held his hand. "I think we should call Mom."

Dr. James said nothing. He merely sat and watched with some unease while Holly found her phone in her purse and dialed the number.

"Hi Mom," she said. "I hope I'm not calling too late. Yes, we're fine. I can't believe it either. Only a few more days." She turned to look at both of us and smiled radiantly while she listened to Margie talk about her visit with Riley and the kids.

"That's sounds wonderful," Holly said. "But I'm calling because Dad is here." She paced around the living room. "Yes, I know it's late. He says hello. He brought us a gift. *Uh huh*. It was Oliver." She paused. "That's right, Josh gave him to me. I can't believe you never mentioned it. You did? I don't remember. Was I only two? Well, that explains it. I know, it was a long time ago. But Dad brought him over and we're just sitting here, talking about Christmas. Yes, that's right. I know. Me, too."

Holly turned to her father and handed him the phone. "She wants to talk to you."

Dr. James's cheeks flushed red. He rose from the sofa, took the phone from her and walked to the kitchen.

Holly sat down across my lap. I cradled her in my arms and kissed the top of her head.

We listened discreetly for a few minutes, then exchanged a look when we heard her father say in a shaky voice, "I'm sorry Margie...Please tell Riley I'm sorry..." Dr. James sat down at my kitchen table and began to weep.

Quietly, Holly and I rose from the chair in the living room and went into the bedroom to give Dr. James some privacy.

Margie, Riley, Lois and the children couldn't get flights out before Christmas, but by some miracle, they were able to fly to Boston and arrive late Christmas Day. It required two vehicles to pick everyone up at the airport, so Holly came with me in my car and Dr. James followed in his.

The whole way there, snow was falling in giant fat flakes that floated in the air like something out of a dream.

"I hope you realize," Holly said, reaching for my hand as we approached the airport, "that none of this would be happening if you hadn't knocked on my door that day."

"Or if I hadn't been shot," I added with a sidelong glance that alluded to a host of other strange and inexplicable things—like the fact that I had seen and spoken to Leah, who died the same night I was shot and who had perhaps decided to stick around long enough to turn me into her final psychiatric case.

Had I needed her help?

Most definitely, yes.

Or maybe she just wanted me to be her messenger.

I won't lie and pretend it was an easy, joyful greeting at the baggage carousel. The children were oblivious to any family tension, of course, and Mrs. James was quick to rush into her husband's arms. Riley and Lois, however, were reserved, as was Dr. James when they shook hands. I suspected the tension and hurt would linger for quite some time to come. Maybe it would never be resolved completely, but at least Riley had agreed to bring his children home for Christmas, so it was a positive first step.

After we collected everyone's bags, we returned to the house where Riley spent many of his most difficult teen years—the house he had not seen in over a decade. He was quiet as we entered and he took his time looking around at all the familiar pieces of furniture, photographs and knick-knacks.

Before we'd departed for the airport, Holly had prepared a traditional turkey dinner which she reheated on the stove when we arrived. The children were rambunctious and misbehaved terribly, but Dr. James somehow managed to bite his tongue and allow sippy-cups in the parlor when it came time to open the gifts.

"Come outside with me?" I said to Holly after Riley and Lois herded the children off to bed. "It's a beautiful night."

She smiled and took my hand.

A few minutes later, we were standing in our coats and boots on the covered veranda by the outdoor tree we had set up that morning.

"It all went well, don't you think?" Holly said, reaching out to touch a golden angel ornament that hung from one of the lower branches.

"It was perfect." I watched her stroll around the tree and felt completely beguiled by her every move.

"The kids had a good time," she added. "Danny liked the toy gas station we picked out for him with all the dinky cars."

"I loved that stuff when I was his age."

She paused to re-arrange a section of lights. I waited until she draped it properly, then I moved a little closer. "There's still one more present, though."

"Really?" She seemed distracted by a twisty length of garland she wanted to straighten. "Who's it for?"

"You."

She stopped what she was doing and looked at me. I tossed my head slightly to indicate a small blue velvet box tied by a silver ribbon to the tallest bough.

She let out a small laugh and I suspected she was about to humor me. "Who's it from?" she asked, refraining from taking it down. She probably couldn't reach it anyway.

"Why don't you open it and find out?" I reached up to free it from the bough, then got down on one knee.

Holly covered her mouth with a hand and smiled.

"Holly James," I said. "I've loved you since the first moment I saw you, twenty-five years ago. I remember it like it was yesterday, and now here we are." I paused to swallow and take a breath. "I think maybe you're the reason I came back from wherever it was I went on the night I was shot, and thank God for that. Or maybe it was Leah who sent me back. Gave me a shove...Maybe she knew you were meant to be my wife."

I opened the box and showed Holly the ring I had chosen just for her—a classic diamond trinity. She gasped and dropped to her knees in front of me.

"Will you marry me?" I asked.

She nodded in a hurry, laughing as I slid the ring onto her finger. "It's so beautiful!" she cried, holding it up to the light shining down on us from the top of the tree.

We both stood up and she wrapped her arms around me. I held her close, closed my eyes and touched my lips to hers.

A moment later, we looked up to admire the decorations on the tree, and listened to the distant sound of carolers somewhere down the street.

"There's something I've been wondering about," Holly said tentatively.

"What is it?"

"When Dad went to your apartment with Oliver in the Christmas box, he said he came home to find the tree all lit up. But didn't we turn off all the lights when we left? I was sure we did."

For a long while, I thought about what she was asking, then I looked up at the angel on top of the tree. "A year ago I would have come up with some sort of rational explanation for that, but after everything that's happened, I'm beginning to accept that maybe some things just happen, and they aren't meant to be explained."

The grandfather clock began to chime from inside the house, but I barely heard a thing as I pulled Holly close and bent my head to kiss her.

Epilogue

⌬

Three years have passed since the day I proposed to my wife. That was the year her family broke apart, but found its way back together again, even stronger than before.

Except for Leah, of course. I'm fairly certain she's moved on to another place now, as I've had no more dreams of her, nor any clear encounters with the afterlife. Although maybe it's arrogant of me to think she's gone just because I can't see her.

Holly tells me she feels her sometimes when she walks into a quiet room at her parents' home on Russell Street, but I wonder if it's just the memory of Leah. Or the love that still exists. Unfortunately, there's nothing concrete about love or the soul. No way to prove either actually exists. You can't touch love or reduce it down to a mathematical equation.

But how odd it is for me to think in those terms when I was once a thick-skinned, uninspired man's man. Holly often calls me "sensitive," which I politely ask her not to say in front of my buddies at the department, especially now that I've been promoted to lieutenant. It's not how they see me or know me, and it's certainly not how I was before the shooting.

It's not that I'm not genuine at work, but they don't know the *real* me. The heart of that man is reserved for Holly alone, and the members of our family.

Maybe it was fate that arranged for Holly and me to meet when we did, otherwise, if she'd known me before, she might never have given me the time of day—which only confirms my belief that everything happens when it's meant to happen.

Dr. and Mrs. James recently celebrated their fortieth anniversary and we all gathered together at their summer house on Cape Cod. Even Riley, Lois and the kids flew in for the party.

Holly graduated from medical school last spring and is now doing exactly what she always dreamed of doing. She's working forensics with the FBI. She still does karate three times a week and I'm her new sparring partner. I'll be testing for my brown belt next year.

As for Robert and his son, Riley...They've come a long way. Robert's counseling has helped a lot, and Riley is no stranger to human weakness, given all that he's seen and heard in the support groups he leads in Billings. He's the most forgiving man I've ever met. Lois is that way, too, but life hasn't been easy on either of them the past few years. They've had their ups and downs.

But haven't we all?

The important thing is to keep getting up each day knowing that everything can turn on a dime. For better or for worse. Sometimes bad things happen, and people will always make mistakes, but isn't that how we learn and grow stronger? That's why we need to treasure each moment of every day, learn how to accept and forgive, and never fear what might be over the horizon, even if it looks dark and cloudy. Because it just might turn out to be the best day of your life.

Questions for Discussion

1. During Josh's description of his childhood experiences from Chapters Eight through Twelve, what passages or images suggest an overlap between Josh's memory of that time in his life, the reality of his near-death experience and Leah's ghostly presence at his bedside?

2. After Josh wakes up in the hospital, were you aware that Leah was a ghostly presence? What clues can you identify that suggest she was not an active resident doctor at the hospital and not a living person? What elements suggest that she *was* a living person? How would you explain these?

3. The issue of the line drawn through the request for a psychiatric consultation in Josh's medical chart is never resolved. Discuss what you believe happened with his chart and why there were no notes about his alleged interviews with Leah.

4. Discuss the author's use of color in the novel when describing the various settings, clothing and events.

5. Discuss the following passage from the end of Chapter Forty-six: "A bluebird landed in a tree across from where we sat. For a long while I sat in Josh's arms, admiring the bird's vivid plumage until she lifted off the branch and flew away again."

6. Have you had a near-death experience, or know another person who has? What was it like for you or them? What do you believe about the phenomenon?

7. Analyze the dreams that Josh has in Chapters Thirty-two, Fifty, and Fifty-four.

8. Do you believe Holly's mother was right to take her husband back so quickly after their separation? Do you believe their marriage has a bright future? Why or why not?

9. Discuss Dr. James as a husband and father. Was there anything to admire about how he conducted himself? Do you believe there is hope that he can change?

Other Books In The Color Of Heaven Series

The COLOR *of* HEAVEN

A deeply emotional tale about Sophie Duncan, a successful columnist whose world falls apart after her daughter's unexpected illness and her husband's shocking affair. When it seems nothing else could possibly go wrong, her car skids off an icy road and plunges into a frozen lake. There, in the cold dark depths of the water, a profound and extraordinary experience unlocks the surprising secrets from Sophie's past, and teaches her what it means to truly live…and love.

Full of surprising twists and turns and a near-death experience that will leave you breathless, this story is not to be missed.

"A gripping, emotional tale you'll want to read in one sitting."
— *New York Times* bestselling author, Julia London

"Brilliantly poignant mainstream tale."
— 4 ½ starred review, *Romantic Times*

The COLOR of DESTINY

Eighteen years ago a teenage pregnancy changed Kate Worthington's life forever. Faced with many difficult decisions, she chose to follow her heart and embrace an uncertain future with the father of her baby – her devoted first love.

At the same time, in another part of the world, sixteen-year-old Ryan Hamilton makes his own share of mistakes, but learns important lessons along the way. Twenty years later, Kate's and Ryan's paths cross in a way they could never expect, which makes them question the possibility of destiny. Even when all seems hopeless, could it be that everything happens for a reason, and we end up exactly where we are meant to be?

The COLOR *of* HOPE

Diana Moore has led a charmed life. She is the daughter of a wealthy senator and lives a glamorous city life, confident that her handsome live-in boyfriend Rick is about to propose. But everything is turned upside down when she learns of a mysterious woman who works nearby – a woman who is her identical mirror image.

Diana is compelled to discover the truth about this woman's identity, but the truth leads her down a path of secrets, betrayals, and shocking discoveries about her past. These discoveries follow her like a shadow.

Then she meets Dr. Jacob Peterson—a brilliant cardiac surgeon with an uncanny ability to heal those who are broken. With his help, Diana embarks upon a journey to restore her belief in the human spirit, and recover a sense of hope - that happiness, and love, may still be within reach for those willing to believe in second chances.

The COLOR of A DREAM

Nadia Carmichael has had a lifelong run of bad luck. It begins on the day she is born, when she is separated from her identical twin sister and put up for adoption. Twenty-seven years later, not long after she is finally reunited with her twin and is expecting her first child, Nadia falls victim to a mysterious virus and requires a heart transplant.

Now recovering from the surgery with a new heart, Nadia is haunted by a recurring dream that sets her on a path to discover the identity of her donor. Her efforts are thwarted, however, when the father of her baby returns to sue for custody of their child. It's not until Nadia learns of his estranged brother Jesse that she begins to explore the true nature of her dreams, and discover what her new heart truly needs and desires…

The COLOR *of* A MEMORY

Audrey Fitzgerald believed she was married to the perfect man - a heroic firefighter who saved lives, even beyond his own death. But a year later she meets a mysterious woman who has some unexplained connection to her husband....

Soon Audrey discovers that her husband was keeping secrets and she is compelled to dig into his past. Little does she know... this journey of self-discovery will lead her down a path to a new and different future - a future she never could have imagined.

The COLOR of LOVE

Carla Matthews is a single mother struggling to make ends meet and give her daughter Kaleigh a decent upbringing. When Kaleigh's absent father Seth—a famous alpine climber who never wanted to be tied down—begs for a second chance at fatherhood, Carla is hesitant because she doesn't want to pin her hopes on a man who is always seeking another mountain to scale. A man who was never willing to stay put in one place and raise a family.

But when Seth's plane goes missing after a crash landing in the harsh Canadian wilderness, Carla must wait for news… Is he dead or alive? Will the wreckage ever be found?

One year later, after having given up all hope, Carla receives a phone call that shocks her to her core. A man has been found, half-dead, floating on an iceberg in the North Atlantic, uttering her name. Is this Seth? And is it possible that he will come home to her and Kaleigh at last, and be the man she always dreamed he would be?

The COLOR *of the* SEASON

Boston cop, Josh Wallace, is having the worst day of his life. First, he's dumped by the woman he was about to propose to, then everything goes downhill from there when he is shot in the line of duty. While recovering in the hospital, he can't seem to forget the woman he wanted to marry, nor can he make sense of the vivid images that flashed before his eyes when he was wounded on the job. Soon, everything he once believed about his life begins to shift when he meets Leah James, an enigmatic resident doctor who somehow holds the key to both his past and his future…

Praise for Julianne MacLean's
Historical Romances

"MacLean's compelling writing turns this simple, classic love story into a richly emotional romance, and by combining engaging characters with a unique, vividly detailed setting, she has created an exceptional tale for readers who hunger for something a bit different in their historical romances."

- BOOKLIST

"You can always count on Julianne MacLean to deliver ravishing romance that will keep you turning pages until the wee hours of the morning."

—Teresa Medeiros

"Julianne MacLean's writing is smart, thrilling, and sizzles with sensuality."

—Elizabeth Hoyt

"Scottish romance at its finest, with characters to cheer for, a lush love story, and rousing adventure. I was captivated from the very first page. When it comes to exciting Highland romance, Julianne MacLean delivers."

—Laura Lee Guhrke

"She is just an all-around wonderful writer, and I look forward to reading everything she writes."

About the Author

Julianne MacLean is a *USA Today* bestselling author of many historical romances, including The Highlander Series with St. Martin's Press and her popular American Heiress Series with Avon/Harper Collins. She also writes contemporary mainstream fiction, and The Color of Heaven was a *USA Today* bestseller. She is a three-time RITA finalist, and has won numerous awards, including the Booksellers' Best Award, the Book Buyer's Best Award, and a Reviewers' Choice Award from Romantic Times for Best Regency Historical of 2005. She lives in Nova Scotia with her husband and daughter, and is a dedicated member of Romance Writers of Atlantic Canada. Please visit Julianne's website for more information and to subscribe to her mailing list to stay informed about upcoming releases.

OTHER BOOKS BY
JULIANNE MACLEAN

The American Heiress Series:
To Marry the Duke
An Affair Most Wicked
My Own Private Hero
Love According to Lily
Portrait of a Lover
Surrender to a Scoundrel

The Pembroke Palace Series:
In My Wildest Fantasies
The Mistress Diaries
When a Stranger Loves Me
Married By Midnight
A Kiss Before the Wedding - A Pembroke Palace Short Story
Seduced at Sunset

The Highlander Series:
Captured by the Highlander
Claimed by the Highlander
Seduced by the Highlander
The Rebel – A Highland Short Story

The Royal Trilogy:
Be My Prince
Princess in Love
The Prince's Bride

Harlequin Historical Romances:
Prairie Bride
The Marshal and Mrs. O'Malley
Adam's Promise

Time Travel Romance
Taken by the Cowboy

Contemporary Fiction:
The Color of Heaven
The Color of Destiny
The Color of Hope
The Color of a Dream
The Color of a Memory
The Color of Love
The Color of the Season

Made in the USA
Lexington, KY
16 October 2015